"You're a very complex man, aren't you, Alex?" Fabia said softly

"What you see is what you get."

"I don't believe that. I've heard that you can be ruthless in business and I've seen you in action in the social scene, remember. All that doesn't tie up with..."

"With the family man? I thought you had more sense than that, Fabia."

"And the women? Do you fool them the way you fool everyone else?"

Helen Brooks lives in Northamptonshire, England, and is married with three children. As she is an active church member, busy housewife and mother, spare time is at a premium, but her hobbies include reading, swimming, gardening and walking her two energetic, inquisitive and very endearing young dogs. Her long-cherished aspiration to write became a reality when she put pen to paper on reaching the age of forty. To date, Helen has written sixteen titles; *And the Bride Wore Black* marks her first appearance in Harlequin Romance.

AND THE BRIDE WORE BLACK
Helen Brooks

Harlequin Books

TORONTO • NEW YORK • LONDON
AMSTERDAM • PARIS • SYDNEY • HAMBURG
STOCKHOLM • ATHENS • TOKYO • MILAN
MADRID • WARSAW • BUDAPEST • AUCKLAND

ISBN 0-373-03350-8

AND THE BRIDE WORE BLACK

Copyright © 1993 by Helen Brooks.

First North American Publication 1995.

CHAPTER ONE

'Now I'm sure if we'd met before I wouldn't have forgotten.'

As the narrowed tawny eyes swept over her in warm appraisal Fabia had the strangest desire to bare her small white teeth in a snarl like a tigress objecting to a proposed mating.

'No...' As the hard, penetrating gaze came to rest on the dark gold silk of her hair the tall, beautifully dressed man in front of her shook his head slowly. 'I definitely wouldn't have forgotten.' He smiled a slow, predatory smile.

She had felt in her bones that this would happen! History had a macabre way of repeating itself at times! Why, oh, why had she been foolish enough to let Joanie persuade her to come here? He waited a moment for her to speak and then gently lifted her small chin with cool, experienced fingers, bringing her violet-blue eyes up to meet his amused gaze. 'Does the vision talk?' he asked mockingly.

It was in that moment of frustrated anger and embarrassment that the idea was born and, once given life, there was no stopping it. 'Well, landsakes, sure I do, honey...' She forced her normally clear warm voice into a harsh nasal twang, taking the accent of a Southern belle, the tone a good few decibels louder than normal. 'Mary-Lou Dixon at your service, honeychild, and I do mean service...'

She saw the shock register for a brief moment in the handsome face and then he recovered magnificently, taking the hand she held out to him with practised ease. 'Are you with anyone?' he asked politely. 'I didn't see——'

She interrupted him archly with a high, shrill little giggle, fluttering her thick eyelashes with an obviously flirtatious flick of her head. 'Well, sweetiepie, ya surely don' think little ole me would be runnin' around alone, now? Snakes alive!' She giggled again, squeezing his hand meaningfully and ignoring his attempts to retrieve it. 'My pa'd be madder than a pig in a poke!'

'Quite...' The unusual gold-flecked eyes had a slightly dazed glaze to them now and she saw him turn his head warily, glancing round the crowded room in hopes of rescue.

Not yet, mister, she thought determinedly, biting back the laughter with difficulty. You're going to squirm for a bit longer yet. 'Now ah just know ya wanna hear all about little ole me...'

She was still holding his hand and he seemed to have resigned himself to the fact that he was well and truly button-holed, for the moment.

'Now do ya know much about the deep South, honey?' she asked loudly as she pulled herself into his side, taking his arm in a way that suggested they had known each other for a good deal longer than two minutes.

'I'm afraid not,' he said quietly, the polite smile stitched on his face with noble fortitude.

Thank goodness for that, she thought delightedly, drawing on all the old films she had seen for the next few minutes as she drew a graphic picture of spoilt, empty-headed women and dashing young men. It was hard work to keep the accent flowing but oh, so enjoyable, she thought silently, to fool such a self-satisfied male chauvinist pig!

She had slowly drawn even closer as she had talked, engineering herself into the circle of his arm so that she was standing side-on, and, just as she was deciding, reluctantly, that she really would have to let him go, she caught sight of a tall, slim brunette watching them with narrowed cat-like eyes, her beautiful face tight with irritation.

The girlfriend? Her mind raced. He had tried to make a move on her when his girlfriend was here? Pay-off time, Mr Cade, she thought coldly.

As the woman moved towards them, her motive clear, Fabia drawled to a halt, looking up into the closed stony face with a sweet little smile of satisfaction. He hadn't liked the last few minutes, he hadn't liked them at all. 'Well, ah mustn' keep ya from all ya other guests now...' She laughed prettily. 'But before ya go, honeychild...' She had reached up and drawn the amazed face down to hers before he realised what was happening, taking his lips in a firm kiss that to anyone watching looked most enjoyable. 'To thank you for such a truly lovely party,' she murmured as she let him go just as the woman reached their sides.

'Alex?' She left them to it as the amusement that was bubbling to the surface threatened to overflow. She couldn't believe he had swallowed the outrageous parody so completely, but then, she reflected thoughtfully, in the world of mindless lackeys and shameless sycophants that he inhabited she doubted if anyone had ever tried to actually *repel* the great man!

Alexander Cade. Her lip curled as she thought of his name. Millionaire a hundred times over, playboy extraordinaire with film-star good looks and a lifestyle to match. She pictured the tall, muscled body clothed immaculately in the best that money could buy, the long—unusually long—rich, shining brown hair cut expertly to lie into his neck in a style that might look effeminate on the average man but on him merely served to emphasise the slanted tawny eyes, straight nose and hard square jaw.

'Handsome you might be but you don't do a thing for me,' she muttered to the tall figure across the far side of the room standing with his back towards her, probably, she suspected gleefully, because he was terrified of catching her eye again. 'And I haven't finished with you yet, Mr Cade, not by a long chalk!'

'Talking to yourself, Fabia?' Joanie's soft brown eyes were crinkled with laughter as she tapped her friend on the shoulder. 'I know you didn't want to come tonight but there must be someone in all this lot to catch your fancy?' She waved expansively at the huge ballroom.

'You must be joking!' Fabia's deep midnight-blue eyes were scathing and Joanie gave a little sigh of resignation. 'And where have you been anyway? You've missed all the fun.'

'Fun?' Joanie's plump face expressed her bewilderment. 'What fun? And I've been in the loo for half an hour. I should never have had that seafood in the nurses' dining-room at lunchtime.'

'Oh, Joanie.' Fabia smiled with a mixture of affection and annoyance at the woebegone expression on Joanie's face. She loved this friend dearly but at times she was sure she had been sent to this earth with the express purpose of providing her life with a little extra turmoil and irritation—like dragging her to this function tonight, for instance.

They had met in their teens when doing A levels at college, Joanie going on to fulfil her ambition to take up nursing and Fabia carving out a promising career in the world of advertising. The first tenuous thread of friendship had developed into a strong supportive bond that neither wished to break, and whenever either one needed assistance it was immediately given, no questions asked. Like tonight, Fabia thought again grimly, but this time Joanie had had no idea what she was asking.

'What fun, anyway?' Joanie repeated interestedly, catching the gleam of devilment in her friend's eyes with a slight feeling of apprehension. Many years of friendship had taught her that Fabia could be a force to be reckoned with. 'What have you done now?'

'Well, you did say if I came and stayed for a couple of hours you'd be satisfied, didn't you?' Fabia said lightly. 'Well—I have and I will, but how I spend that couple of hours is down to me, right?' She smiled sweetly.

'Fabia, I know that look. What have you done?' There was definite anxiety in Joanie's plain face now and Fabia couldn't resist a wicked chuckle at the undisguised panic in her friend's eyes.

'Nothing much,' she answered quietly. 'Just had a little chat with the great Alexander Cade himself. I mean, the whole point in coming to this fiasco was to gaze adoringly at him, wasn't it?'

'Oh, shut up.' Joanie poked her sharply as her plump face turned pink. 'I only wanted to see what he looked like in the flesh, and all these other famous people too. It's one thing to read about them in the papers but quite another to see them face to face.'

'It sure is,' Fabia said disparagingly, glancing round the room with a blatant look of disgust marring her beautiful face. 'I've never seen such a collection of painted dolls in one place, and that's just the men!'

'Oh, you . . .' Joanie's voice died away as she remembered the original start of the conversation. 'What happened, anyway? Did he really talk to you? Oh, Fabia, I wish it were me. Still, I knew no one would take any notice of me, not in this crowd. They're all so——'

'Pathetic!' Fabia cut in savagely. 'Don't run yourself down, Joanie; you'd make ten of any of these clowns.

Can't you see what these people are like, for goodness' sake? Open your eyes for a minute and wipe the stardust out. Most of them are weak and shallow and totally selfish. They aren't fit to wipe your boots.'

'But they're all so beautiful,' Joanie said wistfully, glancing down at her small heavily boned figure with a gesture of longing. 'And slim.'

'Scrawny, half of them,' Fabia returned scornfully.

'Well, it's all right for you,' Joanie said quietly without a trace of jealousy in her voice as she glanced at Fabia's tall, slender shape topped by the mass of long thick blonde hair and vivid blue eyes set like jewels in a flawless skin. 'You'd knock any one of the women here into a cocked hat. Alexander Cade knew that. I bet——'

'Joanie——'

Fabia's concerned voice was cut off as Joanie tapped her on the cheek affectionately. 'Don't worry, I'm not depressing myself, just stating facts. And I do appreciate your coming tonight. I know you didn't want to and I know you'll probably hate every minute but I so wanted to be at something like this just once. When Dr Campbell gave me the tickets after his wife got ill it was like the chance of a lifetime.'

'Well, we couldn't have afforded them,' Fabia agreed wryly. 'What charity is the great Cade donating to anyway?'

'Cancer research,' Joanie said soberly, 'and they sure need it. Anyway——' she gave a little shake of her plump body '—come on, spill the beans, what's happened?'

Her good-natured face got straighter and straighter as Fabia recounted the little episode, until her brown eyes were wide with horror. 'Don't say, it Joanie,' Fabia said warningly as she finished the account. 'I know I shouldn't have, but it was too good to resist. I shall have to keep it up now, of course,' she added with an innocent smile. 'Must be consistent.'

'Fabia, there are times——'

'Stand back and watch me in action.' Before Joanie could stop her Fabia was on her way across the room to where Alexander Cade was deep in conversation with a somewhat austere-looking elderly man, who had an even more severe-looking woman who was clearly his wife by his side. They glanced up as she reached their side and she had to admire Alexander Cade's self-control. She knew he had been avoiding her since their first encounter and she knew she was unwelcome, but he didn't betray his thoughts for a moment.

'Well, hello again,' he said warily, his smile cool as he looked directly into her eyes, and Fabia registered a slight jolt as the full power of that cold tawny gaze swept over her. 'I hope you are enjoying yourself, Miss Dixon?'

'Sure am, honey, but what's with the "Miss Dixon"?' she drawled playfully with a little roguish wink at the dour-faced couple by his side. 'He's a fast mover, this guy,' she continued knowingly as she placed a light hand on the woman's thin arm. 'Just been introduced and he's takin' honey from the flower, but I sure ain't complainin'.' She let her eyes wander over the strong-muscled body saucily, taking care not to meet his eyes which she knew were cold points of steel in the furious face. 'This sure is one hell of a bee.'

'Well, really!' The woman's outraged murmur of disgust was plainly audible to those about them and she caught one or two interested glances in their direction as she became aware of Joanie sidling round to stand in the background. See what a fool he is, Joanie, she thought bitterly to herself, see what fools they all are! His type were all the same, as she had good cause to know. A pretty face and they were into action like stud stallions! But not this time, Mr Cade! Her eyelashes fluttered pertly as she turned to leave. 'Ah must leave ya for a minute, honey-pie,' she murmured slowly into the pregnant silence, 'but don' ya go flirtin' with no more of the girls, ya hear?' She reached up and kissed the edge of the hard mouth before he had time to resist.

'Who is that woman?' The man's clipped voice didn't make any effort to speak quietly and as Joanie took her arm and hurried her away Fabia saw that her friend's eyes were wet with laughter.

'Fabia, you're priceless, but I shouldn't laugh really. What if he ever finds out?'

'Well, he won't, will he?' Fabia said coolly with a little grin. 'We're hardly likely to ever get an invitation to anything like this again!'

'No, I guess not.' Joanie looked longingly at the laden tables of food at one end of the vast ballroom. 'Ready for something to eat?'

'Come on, then,' Fabia said indulgently.

She found to her surprise that she quite enjoyed the rest of the evening. Joanie had to make several trips to the loo but apart from that slight inconvenience the two girls appreciated every moment of the excellent floor-show that had been organised, one singer in particular having a pure, sweet quality to her voice that Fabia could have listened to for hours. She had to admit the deception with Alexander Cade have given her a terrific boost, although she wouldn't probe her feelings beyond that. The whys and wherefores were in the past and best left there.

When the party finally began to break up Fabia contemplated one last attack on the hapless Mr Cade and then decided, albeit reluctantly, that enough was enough. There had been something in that dark gold gaze that she had found disconcerting, and anyway, one thing was sure: he certainly wouldn't forget her in a hurry! She gave a small secretive smile as the thickly carpeted lift whisked her and Joanie and a few other guests down into the discreetly elegant foyer of the sumptuous hotel.

'Could I just make one last visit before the taxi comes? That seafood doesn't want to say die...' Joanie shot off before Fabia could reply and with a little sigh she seated herself in one of the huge soft silk-upholstered chairs that were dotted about the reception area, kicking off her shoes and stretching her toes with a small sigh. This was the sort of place Robin had taken her to. She brought herself upright with a small jerk. Don't think of him, Fabia, she told herself angrily. You haven't wasted a thought on him in months; don't start now! It was because she was tired, she thought grimly, tired and in the sort of place that brought back a host of unwelcome memories.

She heard the man fall before she saw him, the sound of a body hitting the carpet with a dull thud at the same time as a piercing shriek cut through the hushed atmosphere. 'Billy! Oh, Billy! Someone do something, somebody help him.' As the last word died away she had reached the side of the elderly couple who had just come out of the lift, pushing aside the small plump woman who was kneeling by the side of her equally small plump husband. His face was a ghastly caricature of pain, bulbous eyes distended and skin stretched tight over his red face as he gasped for breath.

It looked as though his wife was going into full-blown hysterics and Fabia glanced round quickly at the crowd of interested onlookers that was gathering as she fumbled with his tie. 'Is there a doctor here? Does anyone know how to deal with a heart attack?' Blank silence met her clear sharp voice and, as the man beside her made another strangled gulp for air that ended in a deadly choking sound, she shouted across to the stunned receptionist who was frozen by her desk, 'Get an ambulance, and quickly!'

He had stopped breathing. As she looked down at the twisted face she was aware that all signs of life had stopped and without pausing to think she went into the emergency procedure she had practised so often with Joanie when her friend was taking her nursing examinations. Loosening his tie and ripping open his clothing, she hit down on to the smooth rounded mass of flesh as hard as she possibly could, hearing the gasp of shock from the crowd gathered round them through the ringing in her ears. The wife increased her screaming at the second blow to her husband's chest and Fabia spared a second to push her aside. 'Will you be quiet? You aren't helping.'

'You're killing him!' At the third blow the woman tried to drag Fabia from her husband's side and then through her concentration she was aware of someone holding the unfortunate woman out of range and talking to her in a deadly quiet voice. Whatever was said worked, as the screams were shut off as though by magic.

On the fifth blow there was a great intake of air from the supine figure and a mingled gasp of relief from the onlookers, who had entered into this battle of life or death wholeheartedly now. Fabia continued to crouch by his side without taking her eyes off his dazed face, talking to him in a low, reassuring tone as he struggled to survive. He stopped breathing once more before the ambulance crew arrived but this time only one hard punch was needed to jolt the reluctant heart into action again, and as they whisked him out to the ambulance one of the crew patted Fabia swiftly on the shoulder. 'Well, done, lass. It was lucky for him you were around.'

It was all over in a second, and as Fabia sank back on her heels into the ankle-deep carpet she was suddenly aware that her hand was throbbing as though she had thumped a brick wall and her head was pounding. 'Oh...' For a moment everything faded in a misty haze.

'OK, folks, the show's over.' As a pair of hard male hands grasped her under her arms, drawing her carefully to her feet, the attentive audience melted away and the vast room once again took on the refined subdued murmur that was customary in such elegant surroundings.

It wasn't until she had been lowered on to the edge of the chair she had vacated a few frantic minutes ago that Fabia rallied sufficiently to raise her eyes, realising that the same voice that had taken charge of the screaming wife so capably earlier was now taking charge of her.

She froze in horror as Alexander Cade stared back at her silently, his strange tawny eyes glittering with unholy fire and his dark face set in lines of deadly cold anger. 'Yours, I think?' As he dangled her shoes in front of her white face a screaming blackness caused her ears to ring and his shape to blur into a tall shadow, and although he moved quickly with a muttered oath he was too late to save her from sliding into a graceful heap at his feet in a dead faint.

'What did you do to her?' She came to in disorientated panic to hear Joanie's soft voice whispering seemingly in her ear. 'What on earth did you do to her?'

'I didn't do anything, you stupid girl.' She recognised the bitingly frosty voice immediately and gave a little groan as she remembered where she was. This was all she needed!

She opened dazed eyes to see Joanie's anxious face two inches from her own. 'Are you all right?'

'Of course she isn't all right.' Joanie was plucked from her vision and a large balloon glass of brandy held in front of her nose. 'Drink that.' The tone was uncompromisingly severe with not a trace of warmth in its arctic depths. 'Now.'

The neat alcohol burnt as it hit her stomach but its reviving power was immediate, and as the colour came back into her face she became aware that she was lying on a remarkably uncomfortable leather sofa in what she presumed was the manager's office.

'Can you sit up?' the hard voice asked coldly above her head.

'Perhaps she shouldn't, we don't know——'

'Look, Miss…?' The two words held intense irritation.

'Fletcher. Joanie Fletcher.' Fabia detected a tremor in Joanie's soft voice and her hackles rose immediately.

'Look, Miss Fletcher, your friend just rendered somewhat extreme first aid on a poor unfortunate man who had the temerity to have a heart attack in front of her, owing to which, among other things, I should think he now has several broken ribs to contend with. If you'd seen what I'd seen you wouldn't be at all surprised at her collapse. I think the man's wife will need psychiatric care for some considerable time——'

'You lying hound!' The fierce adrenalin pumping vigorously through her system banished the last remains of faintness as she swung her feet off the sofa and rose in one swift leap. 'How dare you? I——'

'How dare *I*?' The incredulous note in the icy voice checked her flow of words and as she gazed into the livid countenance towering above her Fabia knew a moment of pure stomach-twisting fear. 'You ask *me* how I dare?' Joanie moved silently to her side in unspoken support, her plump round face as white as a sheet and her hands stretched out imploringly.

'Mr Cade, this isn't what you think——'

He cut off Joanie's anxious voice with a sharply raised hand without taking his eyes off Fabia's face. 'Don't insult my intelligence with excuses, Miss Fletcher, and keep quiet. Do you understand?' The last three words were a bark and now Fabia pushed Joanie to one side as she moved directly in front of him, glaring defiantly right up into his face, while a small part of her mind wondered at this change in him. There was no trace of the elegant, laconic man who had been present all evening. The cool charmer, the enigmatic philanderer, all the things that made up Alexander Cade had disappeared and in their place was a dangerously angry man with blazing eyes and a hard cruel mouth. Why hadn't she noticed his mouth before? she thought faintly. Maybe that was more an indication of the real man than all the glossy camouflage? But no, she shook her head mentally. He was just mad at being made to look such a complete and utter fool. Which he was.

'Why the little charade all evening?' The grim voice was stiff now and she had the impression he was exercising great self-control in speaking quietly. 'What was the point of all that?'

For a brief second she thought about trying to placate him, offer him an excuse that would be more acceptable than the bald truth, and then her spirit rebelled against the deception. He might be the king-pin in his world but not in hers! Oh, no, not in hers, she thought furiously.

'Because I'm sick to death of your type of man, Mr Cade,' she said clearly, her voice firm and strong. 'You think your money can buy anything and anyone and you control your little empire like a big fat spider drawing people into your web. You are vain and you're selfish and probably over-sexed too! What did it feel like to be the hunted for a change? To be backed into a corner by someone who repulsed you? Fun, was it?'

He listened to her angry tirade with narrowed eyes and folded arms and strangely, in view of the insults she had just hurled at him, seemed calmer when she had finished than when she had begun. 'What was his name?' he asked softly when she paused for breath.

'What?' Unconsciously she took a step backwards, her wide eyes darkening to midnight-blue and her breath catching in her throat. 'I don't know what you're talking about.'

'No?' He was smiling now, a cruel hard calculating smile, a smile that robbed her of speech and seemed to strip her bare until she had the crazy notion he could read her mind. 'I think you do. And I was his substitute, eh? A nice convenient deputy ready to hand whom you could vent your venom on and make a laughing-stock of.'

'Look, no one knows, Mr Cade.' Joanie came back into the conversation after one glance at Fabia's white, shocked face.

'*I* know!' The words were an explosion of the fury he was keeping in check and Fabia flinched instinctively as she took another step backwards. What had she done? What *had* she done? 'You're going to pay for this, my golden-haired little beauty.'

The words were low and soft but with such acrimony in their depths that she shuddered as a shiver snaked down her spine. He looked like one of the old Greek gods as he stood there in front of them, the harsh artificial light directly over his head catching the tawny gleam in his dark brown hair and turning his eyes to pure gold, his tanned skin and great height adding to the impression of a blazingly beautiful golden statue come to life with a mission of revenge and destruction. He was... terrifying.

'Oh, I feel sick...' As Joanie slumped against her Fabia's arm instinctively reached out to support her. 'I've got to get to a loo again, Fabia.' She bowed her head helplessly.

'I don't believe this.' Alexander Cade's contemptuous voice bit through the air. 'What game are we playing now?'

'It's no game.' There was no mistaking the ring of truth in Fabia's indignant voice as she cradled Joanie in her arms. 'She's been ill on and off all night. She's a nurse, for goodness' sake. Don't you think when that man collapsed she would have helped if she hadn't been . . . indisposed? She——'

'All right, all right.' He waved his hand irritably. 'Help her to the ladies' powder-room but first . . .' He pressed a bell on the wall and immediately a small middle-aged man opened the door leading out into the reception hall, making Fabia think he had been listening outside. 'There you are, Swinton. Escort these . . . ladies to the powder-room and then wait outside so they won't get lost on the way back. OK?' His voice was icily controlled.

'OK, sir.' The man gave a quick nod, the ghost of a smile touching his lips as he turned to Fabia.

'And Swinton?'

'Yes, sir?'

'Tell the manager he can have his office back now. I won't be needing it any longer. These ladies are going to return upstairs.' The grim voice was chilling.

'Very good, sir.' Swinton gestured for them to follow him.

'You can't——' Fabia's furious voice was cut off as Joania moaned quietly by her side, her voice a soft whimper.

'Please . . .'

'OK, you're all right, don't worry.' All her attention was concentrated on Joanie as they left the room and she didn't even glance at the tall silent figure standing to one side of the doorway, his arms folded in silent scrutiny.

'Quick, Fabia!' As the door of the large and very luxurious powder-room closed behind them Joanie jerked herself off Fabia's arm and pulled her over to the row of pink shell-shaped washbasins lining one velvet-embossed wall. 'Come on.'

As Joanie lifted the hem of her shiny, sweetie-paper-style evening dress, exposing two rounded plump knees, Fabia stared at her in amazement.

'What on earth——?'

'Come on, you idiot! We haven't got much time.' With an agility that belied her stout build, her friend had climbed on to the veneered wood that supported the vanity unit before Fabia could blink, reaching up and loosening the catch to the narrow frosted window and peering outside carefully. 'I thought so. This leads into the yard where they keep the dustbins and there's a side door at one end into the street. *Come on*, Fabia!'

'You aren't seriously thinking of climbing through that little thing, are you?' Fabia looked up into Joanie's flushed face in horror. 'And I thought you felt ill?'

'And I thought I was supposed to be the dim one,' Joanie muttered irritably. 'Face facts, Fabia. There's a man out there who's loaded like a lethal weapon and he's definitely gunning for you. Now you can try sweet reason on him but I wouldn't give much for your chances.' Fabia pictured the narrowed cat-like eyes and cruel mouth and nodded slowly. 'The only other alternative as I see it is to remove the target from the firing-range.'

'You mean run away,' Fabia said flatly.

'I *mean*,' Joanie took a deep breath that vibrated with impatience, 'that just for once you should admit you're in a situation you can't handle and do the sensible thing. He's got more clout than a field full of turnips!' Fabia reflected wryly that in moments of extreme stress Joanie's country upbringing became more obvious. 'You can't beat him so let's make a dignified retreat!'

'Dignified?' Fabia stared aghast at the small window. 'And what if someone comes in?'

'Someone will in a minute,' Joanie said grimly, 'and he's about six feet four and hopping mad. Don't think about it, just take notice of me for once in your life, and *come on*!'

As Fabia joined Joanie in her precarious perch she had the insane urge to break into hysterical laughter. This wasn't at all how she had visualised finishing the evening, she reflected wryly, as she hoisted the soft blue silk of her evening dress about her waist, exposing the full length of her slim beautifully shaped legs to the blank gaze of the expensively ornate mirror opposite. 'Hang on a minute.' She jumped down again just as Joanie prepared to launch herself out of the window, and heard her friend's exasperated sigh as she rummaged frantically in her tiny evening-bag.

'What on earth are you doing, woman?' Joanie whispered nervously. 'You haven't got time to titivate.'

'I'm just leaving a little goodbye note,' she said softly as she wrote boldly on the clear glass with her lipstick. 'I don't want him to think I'm a complete chicken.'

'Who cares what he thinks?' Joanie muttered crossly. 'If you don't hurry up he'll be able to tell you himself.' She peered at what Fabia had written and groaned softly. 'There are times——'

'I know, I know.' Fabia climbed up beside her again and gave her a little nudge. 'Go on, then, be careful.' She heard a tiny muffled grunt as Joanie slid out of the window and then it was her turn. As the cold night air met her hot face a sense of adventure stirred her blood in a way it hadn't been stirred since she was a child. 'This is fun, isn't it?' she murmured as she landed beside Joanie against the brick wall. 'Cowboys and Indians!'

'Oh, wonderful,' Joanie said sarcastically as she glanced nervously around the small dark courtyard. 'And guess who'll end up with an arrow in her back if we're not careful!'

As they tiptoed across the shadowed and none too clean yard Fabia found Joanie was gripping her arm tightly and glanced at her friend's set face as she patted her hand comfortingly. 'Don't worry, we're nearly home and dry.'

'You're enjoying this, aren't you?' Joanie accused softly. 'You're actually enjoying it.'

'I am rather,' Fabia agreed lightly, opening the bolted door into the narrow side-street and looking warily about her. The lights and traffic of the main thoroughfare a few yards away spelt safety and it was with a sense of anticlimax that she found herself hurrying, a few minutes later, along the brightly lit street and away from the hotel.

'Taxi!' As they collapsed into the back seat of the big London taxi Joanie leant back against the upholstered plastic with a small sigh, stretching her small plump legs wearily.

'What a night!'

'I thought you enjoyed it?' Fabia said cheerfully as she glanced at Joanie out of the corner of her eye. 'It made a change.'

'It did that all right.' Joanie's voice was loaded with feeling. 'And I'm dying for the loo again, and it's for real this time!'

It was an hour or two later as Fabia lay quietly in bed, hands behind her head and sleep a million miles away, that she felt the laughter that had been bubbling below the surface all evening begin to emerge as she pictured Alexander Cade's face when he saw the message she had scribbled on the mirror. 'Bye for now, sweet thing—catch ya later.' He wouldn't like it! She hugged herself as she giggled helplessly at the understatement. He wouldn't like it at all. To be made a fool of twice in the same evening; it would drive him crazy!

When the paroxysm of laughter had died away a slight feeling of disquiet took its place. How crazy would it drive him? Crazy enough to try and find her? She shook her head slowly, silky strands of corn-gold hair drifting across her face in a soft veil. It wouldn't matter if he did. He didn't even know her name. She relaxed again, snuggling further down under the duvet as she tried to empty her mind preparatory for sleep. She knew plenty about him; he was hardly ever out of the newspapers and glossy magazines with a different model-type girl gracing his arm, and no doubt his bed, each time. But he knew nothing about her. A smile touched her full pink lips as her eyelids grew heavy. And that was just the way she wanted it.

CHAPTER TWO

THE radio was blaring forth a carol as Fabia whisked two eggs into fluffy lightness for the omelette she was preparing to accompany the solitary pork chop sizzling in its own juices under the grill.

The November day had a starkness that spoke of snow and it was the first of December tomorrow, two whole weeks since that eventful night. So why did her mind keep harping back to Alexander Cade? And why did everything seem so dull at the moment?

She glanced round the bright cheerful kitchen of her tiny flat. She had been so thrilled when she had first acquired this, a home of her own, five years ago. And she still was, really. It was just that... She paused in her thoughts. What was it exactly?

The doorbell interrupted her musing, chiming shrilly across the last chords of 'Once in Royal David's City', and she switched off the music as she went to answer the door. Not Brian again, she thought irritably as she glanced at her wristwatch. This was about the time her neighbour got home from work and lately he had intensified his relentless pursuit of her, her snubs sliding off his thick skin unheeded. For some reason he considered himself a special gift to womankind although she couldn't understand why; the thick lips and greedy pig-like eyes did absolutely nothing for her except to create a slight feeling of nausea.

'Joanie!' As she opened the door and saw Joanie standing outside, her face as white as a sheet, she moved forward with an exclamation of concern. 'What's wrong?'

'Fabia, I'm sorry, I had to——'

'It would seem your friend is feeling somewhat unwell again.' For a second all time was suspended in a weird kind of time-lock as her stunned eyes watched Alexander Cade's lean, tall body move to stand just behind Joanie in the doorway. 'Do you know how many nurses with the surname of Fletcher there are in London hospitals and the surrounding districts?' he asked conversationally, his eyes registering satisfaction at her shock. 'Of course I had to include private nursing homes and suchlike on the list. One has to be thorough.' His smile was chilling as his eyes swept insultingly down her body.

'Now look here, Mr Cade——'

He cut off her shaking voice as quickly as he shed the mantle of mildness. 'But I am looking . . . Fabia, I think Miss Fletcher just called you? An improvement on Mary-Lou, I would agree. I've done nothing *but* look over the last two weeks, incidentally. You've cost me a considerable amount of time and effort, not to mention money, Miss . . . ?'

'Grant.' Her voice was flat. 'Fabia Grant.'

'A delightful name.' The icy eyes narrowed. 'And now, Miss Fabia Grant, you will explain exactly what the hell you have been playing at.' He turned to Joanie abruptly. 'My car will take you home, Miss Fletcher. Kindly tell my chauffeur to return here for me.'

'Please, Mr Cade.' Joanie spoke faintly into the heavy atmosphere. 'It was just a joke, a silly joke. Fabia didn't mean——'

'A joke?' The dark voice expressed exaggerated disappointment. 'And here was I thinking my fatal charm had won out after all in view of your farewell.'

'What?' Fabia stared at him for a moment in bewilderment.

' "Bye for now, sweet thing—catch you later".' As he repeated the words she had found so amusing at the time a slow shiver ran down Fabia's spine and she heard Joanie groan softly. 'Well, you wanted to catch me, Miss Grant, and now you have.' The tawny eyes held her fast. 'And what are you going to do with me?' As she stared at him, temporarily dumbstruck, he inclined his head towards Joanie. 'And please tell your friend to avail herself of my offer. The car is waiting for her.'

'It's all right, Joanie, you go,' Fabia muttered slowly as Joanie shook her head at Alexander Cade's words.

'No, I can't leave you, I——'

'You will leave now.' He turned the full force of his piercingly cold eyes on Joanie—she shrank back slightly and the numbness that had taken hold of Fabia melted as a tide of furious rage washed over her, bringing her snapping upright on her heels.

'Don't you dare talk to her like that. You have no right——'

'Don't talk to me of "rights", Miss Grant,' he snarled softly. 'You lost me a very important business deal with that little act you put on at my reception, so don't talk of "rights".' He turned to Joanie, his manner milder. 'You can go, Miss Fletcher. I have no intention of harming your friend in any way but I am determined to speak to her, and in private.'

'Fabia?'

'Go on, Joanie.' She pushed her gently towards the waiting lift. 'I'll be all right.'

As the doors closed on Joanie's white, troubled face Fabia looked up at Alexander Cade, her eyes huge in her pale face, and in the same instant he moved forward, taking her in his arms before she had time to protest.

'Well, sweet thing,' he drawled mockingly, his eyes fiery, 'as I said, you've caught me. Let's see if the promise in that delectable body holds true.'

When his mouth fastened on hers she was too surprised at first to feel anything but furious outrage, and as she struggled helplessly in his iron grip she was aware of the wicked chuckle deep in his throat as he moulded her softness into his body. She wasn't quite sure when a subtle awareness of him as a man—and what a man!—crept into her consciousness, but when it did she renewed her efforts, struggling violently as a warm sweet languor threatened to take over her limbs.

'Stop it.' He raised his mouth a fraction to admonish her. 'You asked for this—enjoy it.'

Her words of protest were lost as the firm hard lips took her mouth again and she suddenly realised he wouldn't let her go till she submitted. As she forced herself to become still in his arms the dark head raised again, and this time there was a glow of satisfaction in the tawny eyes.

'Good girl.' His voice was bitingly mocking. 'I can see you're catching on already.'

'You're a brute.' Her voice was annoyingly breathless but she couldn't help it. She couldn't remember when a kiss had affected her like that.

'Now, now, no insults please.' He took a step backwards and smiled tauntingly. 'You had a head start on me, after all. I seem to remember you've kissed me twice already?'

'That was different.' She glared at him angrily as her shoulders squared for battle. 'And you know it.'

'The hell I do!' There was only anger in his voice now.

She glared at him helplessly. 'I suppose you'd better come in.'

'How kind.' He followed her into the small lounge, his eyes shooting to the window and then back to her angry face. 'And just remember we're three floors up now. The windows are hardly conducive to flight, unless you're a bird, that is, of the feathered kind.' There was a hard thread of steel in the contemptuous drawl but nothing could have stopped Fabia's rage from spilling over as she looked into the handsome cruel face.

'I suppose you think you've been very clever!' She took a step forward as she spoke, her voice a low hiss and her eyes glittering blue fire, but he merely smiled slowly, totally unperturbed.

'No more than usual.' He let his eyes wander down her body in taunting contempt. 'But it's you who should be getting the Oscar, isn't it? Such a riveting performance and so well executed. You had us all on the edge of our seats.'

She glared at him furiously. 'Did I, indeed?'

'You sure did.' The slanted eyes fixed firmly on to hers. 'And none more so than Mr Hymes.'

'Mr Hymes?' She stared at him blankly. 'I don't remember anyone called Mr Hymes.'

'No?' He smiled thinly. 'Well, Mr and Mrs Hymes certainly will remember you for a long, long time. Your little charade cost me a vital business contract and irreplaceable good will. I'd been setting that deal up for six months and you blew it in as many minutes. They are as strait-laced as they come and didn't appreciate your particular brand of... entertainment.'

'Oh.' She tried to remember exactly what she had said and then winced as she did so. 'I see.'

'"I see"?' He glared at her. 'Is that the best you can do?'

'Look, I can explain——' Fabia stopped suddenly. No, she couldn't explain, not even to herself. What madness had possessed her to take on someone as powerful as Alexander Cade?

'I'm almost tempted to let you try,' he said smoothly.

He was aware of her discomfiture and loving every minute of it, Fabia thought furiously, her eyes shooting daggers.

'Instead we'll cut through the nonsense and I'll tell you what I've come for. But not here.' He glanced round him as though her home was distasteful to him. Which it probably was, she thought bitterly, in view of the indulgent splendour in which he normally lived.

'If you've got anything to say to me you say it here and now, Mr Cade,' Fabia said angrily. 'And for the record I'm not going anywhere with you. Not now, not ever.'

'Think again.' The two words were loaded with menace.

'On your bike, mister!' She would not be intimidated or threatened in her own home. She would not!

'"On your bike"?' He repeated her words with a trace of amusement lightening the dark face. 'It's been years since I had a bike, Miss Grant,' he said mockingly.

'Now that I can believe,' she said stonily. 'Born with a silver spoon, the original spoiled brat, am I right?'

'Would you believe me if I said no?' he asked in a tone to match hers, his eyes narrowing as she shook her head firmly. 'No, I thought not, so I'll save my breath.' He walked through to the kitchen, turning off the grill as he did so and peering at the charred remains of the chop. 'Was that your dinner?'

'This *is* my dinner, yes,' she said coldly. 'Not quite up to your pretentious standards of smoked caviare and oysters maybe, but it suits me.'

'What a nasty prickly little inverted snob you are, Miss Grant,' he said slowly. 'Are you always this obnoxious?' His eyes wandered in insulting appraisal over her slender figure, resting for a moment on the full high breasts before continuing up to her hot angry face. 'Such a shame, when the exterior promises so much,' he added meaningfully.

'I don't promise anything,' she said furiously, longing to reach up and smack the coolness from his handsome face but not quite having the courage. How dared he? *How dared he*? He had done nothing but criticise her home since he came in and now he was doing the same to her.

'Look, it's obvious you think this place is a dump, so why don't you just leave?' she said flatly, forcing all emotion out of her voice by sheer will-power. 'You've made your point, you're omnipotent, the all-powerful one, you found me against all the odds and I'm suitably chastised.' Her hand moved unconsciously to her bruised lips. 'Can't we leave it at that?'

'I haven't made my point at all,' he said after a long moment of silence. 'And I do not think your flat is a...dump, I think you so quaintly termed it.' He glanced round the light painted walls and the windowsill full of flowering plants before turning to inflict the full gaze of his piercing eyes on her again. 'And I repeat, I wish to speak to you in private. That is no slur on your home, merely the wishes of a hungry man who wants to discuss a particular matter in private at the same time as filling his stomach. I take it you wouldn't like to cook me dinner?' She glared at him silently. 'No, I thought not.' He smiled coldly. 'Then you take the alternative. Yes?'

She still didn't speak.

'We can either do this the hard way or the easy way, Miss Grant,' he said after a full minute of taut silence had elapsed. 'I am not going to abduct you if you allow me to buy you dinner, I am not going to threaten you or mistreat you in any way, in fact I am not going to deal with you at all as you deserve.'

The last was said so matter-of-factly that for a moment she missed its import, and then she flushed angrily as his words registered. 'How do I know I can trust you?' she asked slowly. 'That you won't try to kiss me again?'

'You don't.' He leant lazily against the door as he spoke, his tawny eyes gleaming oddly. 'But this is what is called taking the consequences, Miss Grant. Unpleasant, maybe, but if you play games then you have to accept the forfeit. Understand?'

'I don't understand any of this,' she snapped angrily as she snatched the grill off the stove and placed it in water, opening the kitchen window to let the pungent smell of burnt meat fade. 'Not any of it!'

'No, maybe not,' he said complacently. 'It's for me to explain and you to listen. Now, get your coat and we'll go. Swinton should be back with the car by now.'

She marched past him, through the lounge and into the bedroom without a word. 'Look on it as a bonus, Miss Grant.' The hated voice followed her. 'You'll be fed and watered.'

'I'm not a dog,' she said stiffly as she marched out of the bedroom with her coat slung over her arm, and then blushed hotly at the look on his face as his eyes ran over her again.

'That you aren't, Fabia Grant,' he agreed softly, 'that you aren't.' His gaze fastened lingeringly on her swollen lips.

As they left the flat Brian was just entering his, next door, a bottle of cheap wine under his arm. The small eyes took in the situation as Alexander Cade took her arm. The feel of his hand through the soft material of her dress was disconcerting and she had to stop herself sighing audibly with relief when he loosened his hold as they waited for the lift, helping her on with her coat without speaking, his face expressionless.

Within moments they were downstairs in the somewhat dour entrance hall and as she walked by his side towards the big glass doors she found her legs were shaking along with a distinct trembling in the pit of her stomach, and it wasn't all due to fright, she acknowledged silently. Away from the affected, subservient hangers-on who were part of his entourage and the opulent sophisticated surroundings in which she had seen him, the sheer maleness of the man came across in a virile potency that was almost tangible. He was tall, very tall, and the big black overcoat that he wore made him seem even larger, his shoulders broad and powerful under the expensive cloth. His hair was brushing the collar of the coat, gleaming with rich life against the dark material, and he exuded a sensual, intoxicating, dominant mastery that made her feel helplessly feminine even as she chided herself for her weakness. He wasn't anything like Robin. As the thought came unbidden into her mind her foot-steps faltered and his hand came out instantly to steady her. 'All right?'

'I'm fine.' She flinched from his touch and his hand fell immediately to his side, but apart from a slight tight-ening of the hard mouth he displayed no emotion at all, his face closed against her. He was suddenly a different man, icy and very distant.

'The car's over here.' She looked across the dark road to where a magnificent Bentley was waiting regally in the shadows, the man he had called Swinton sitting in the driving seat. 'Shall we...?' He took her arm again as they crossed the street and she forced herself to display no reaction to his touch even as her mouth dried with a mixture of fear and excitement. What on earth had she got herself into? He was right out of her league in every way. And that kiss!

'Now, Miss Grant.' As she seated herself in the spacious interior he slid in beside her, tapping on the glass that separated them from Swinton and indicating to him to drive on when he turned round. 'A couple of things we need to get straight before I take you for a meal.'

'You needn't take me for a meal,' she protested quickly, 'I really don't——'

'The first thing.' It was just as though she hadn't spoken, and she subsided against the soft leather, her senses reeling as she caught a whiff of deliciously expensive aftershave. 'I shall call you Fabia and you will call me Alex. OK?'

'OK.' Her voice was weak and she heard it with a trace of anger sharpening her mind. Don't go all soft and pathetic now, Fabia, she told herself tightly. You're going to need all your wits about you tonight. 'And the other thing?' she said more loudly, her voice firm. Sexual magnetism was wasted on her!

'The other thing is that, in spite of having every reason for the contrary, I am not your enemy, Fabia. Got it?' The sound of her name on his lips caused her heart to pound crazily but she kept her face bland as she nodded quietly, not trusting herself to speak. 'I don't know what prompted you to act as you did and I won't pretend I like it——' the deep voice harshened a little '—but I'm not here tonight for revenge so you can relax a little.' He glanced down at her hands bunched in two tight fists in her lap, and as she caught his glance hot colour raced across her cheekbones in humiliating awareness of how easily he read her mind. She hated him, she really did!

'What are you here for, then?' she asked stiffly. 'There must be hundreds of women all too ready to fall into your lap, Mr—Alex.'

'Undoubtedly,' he agreed laconically. 'Unfortunately wealth is a powerful aphrodisiac to certain women, Fabia, which can prove ... irritating at times.'

'Can it?' she asked cynically, her gaze resting on the classic profile as he stared straight ahead. She doubted if he had ever needed any help in that area in his life.

'It can.' He glanced at her, catching her wide blue eyes with his sharp gaze. 'Now correct me if I'm wrong but I rather suspect that, although you may have many failings, that is not one of them?' His voice was full of mocking amusement.

She nodded slowly. 'I've nothing against money and what it can buy, it's only the love of money that I find repellent.'

'Quite.' The light brown gaze intensified. 'You are quite right in your assumption that I was born into wealth, as it happens—extreme wealth. However, I was not spoiled.' She lowered her eyes but not before he had seen the disbelieving gleam in their dark blue depths. 'You don't believe me?'

'No, I don't,' she answered frankly. 'You probably wouldn't know what a normal childhood was, so how can you say for sure that you weren't spoiled? And your lifestyle now is so outrageous, I don't think——'

'Outrageous?' He looked at her keenly. 'Do you really believe everything you read in the sordid little tabloids? I would have thought a woman of your intelligence would have kept an open mind on such sensationalism, but maybe that was before?'

'Before?' Her voice expressed her puzzlement. 'Before what?'

'Before whoever hurt you so badly left.' As the hot colour flared under her high cheekbones he turned away to look out of the window. 'I'm not ashamed of my wealth, Fabia,' he continued quickly before she had a chance to speak. 'I make it work for me and I use it wisely, but because of the amount I have any anonymity is merely a pipe-dream.'

'Oh, come on,' she said sceptically. 'Do you really expect me to believe that all those fabulous parties and different women for each day of the week are a figment of the Press's imagination? And you love every minute.' Her voice was bitter now. 'You know you do.'

'I don't expect you to believe anything,' he said quietly. 'It's not important anyway. I was merely trying to give you a little background information in view of what I intend to ask you later. One thing.' He paused and looked at her hard. 'I was not spoilt as a child, not at all. I don't know if you are aware of it but my parents were killed when I was three months old and I inherited everything. I was brought up by my paternal grandmother, who is a quite exceptional old lady. If you met her you would understand.' He moved to the edge of his seat as the car drew to a smooth halt. 'We've arrived—shall we ...?'

'Please.' She caught hold of his coat-sleeve as he opened the door and he turned in surprise. 'Stop the cat-and-mouse game. What do you want from me?'

'All in good time.' He climbed out of the car and moved round to open her door, helping her out into the busy London street carefully. 'Give us a couple of hours, Swinton.' Swinton nodded blandly and the big car nosed gently into the traffic again to the usual blaring of horns from impatient city traffic.

The restaurant was quietly elegant and discreetly lit, full of secluded alcoves and attentive waiters who greeted Alex with an almost reverential respect that he seemed quite oblivious to. But he would be, wouldn't he? Fabia thought bitterly; he was used to this every day of his life. 'Your usual table, Mr Cade?' The manager appeared from nowhere, almost touching his forelock as he escorted them to a small table, out of sight of the general diners, already set for two with a large bowl of hothouse orchids gracing the snow-white linen cloth. Fabia sat down gingerly, hardly daring to breathe.

'An aperitif?' Alex looked across at her, the manager standing to attention by his side, and she suddenly rebelled against the ostentation, the ostentation that had trapped and degraded her all those years ago.

'No, thank you.' She smiled sweetly up at the waiter hovering at the manager's elbow. 'Could I have a glass of water, please?'

'A glass of water?' The young waiter was open-mouthed but the manager stepped in smoothly, his voice expressionless and his face bland.

'Certainly, miss. And your usual champagne cocktail, Mr Cade?'

Alex hadn't taken his eyes off her during the little exchange and now he smiled slowly, his face enigmatically intent. 'I think I'll join Miss Grant, Xavier. Could I have ice and lemon in mine, please?'

'Er—yes, Mr Cade, certainly.' From the delighted expression on the waiter's face Fabia assumed it wasn't often the young lad had seen his prestigious superior at a loss for words but it was happening now. Xavier opened his mouth to speak, closed it again and then backed away silently, clicking his fingers at the waiter who set a gold menu-card in front of them before quickly following his boss.

Fabia opened her menu silently, a pink flush on her cheeks, and glanced down the contents with a feeling of apprehension. French. She might have known. She glanced up to find Alex's eyes still fixed on her. 'Would you like me to order for you? There are some dishes that are always exceptional here.' He was giving her an easy get-out but she didn't take it, her eyes steady on his as she stared into their tawny depths. He knew. He knew she couldn't speak French.

'Yes, please, this is all double Dutch to me.' There was a slightly defiant tilt to her chin as she spoke and he smiled that slow deep smile again, his eyes warm as they flickered over her beautiful face. She was feeling distinctly under-dressed for her surroundings, which didn't help, the pencil-slim black skirt and heavy gold blouse that had been just right for the office lamentably out of place next to the exclusive creations most of the women were wearing. Still, no one could see her here. She relaxed slightly. And it was his fault! If he was embarrassed by her it was his fault.

Alex didn't seem at all embarrassed, leaning back in his chair with his hands on the table, his dark face implacable and his eyes alive with laughter. 'Did you enjoy that?'

'What?' She knew exactly what he meant and glared at him as he gave a soft chuckle.

'Poor Xavier, and he so prides himself on his creative cocktails; you've quite ruined his night.'

'You didn't have to join me, you could have had what you wanted,' she said tartly, her eyes flashing.

'I wanted to join you, Fabia,' he said softly as all amusement left his face. 'I've got exactly what I wanted.' There was a strange expression on his face and she stared at him uncertainly for a moment or two before he leant forward to touch her cheek with the tip of one finger, his eyes unreadable. 'I thought so—soft as silk.'

'Don't!' She jerked back so violently from his touch that she almost knocked the glass of water that the waiter was presenting over her shoulder out of his hand.

'Sorry.' She smiled up at the young lad quickly. 'My fault.'

'Thank you, miss.' He placed the beautifully cut crystal wine glass in front of her carefully. 'I was told to put it in this glass, is that all right, miss?' She grinned wryly and he gave an answering smile, communicating without words, totally on her wave-length.

'Well, if that's the best there is I suppose it will have to do,' she said.

'I wondered how you'd look with a real smile and I know now, don't I?' There was a note in Alex's voice that made her raise her head sharply in surprise but his face was quite expressionless apart from a strange glow in the piercing eyes as he held her glance with his. 'Do I have to take up waiting at tables to get under that beautiful skin?'

'Don't be ridiculous,' she said coldly, forcing her gaze not to drop before his.

'Ridiculous ... ?' He leant forward again and lifted a strand of hair with one finger. 'I don't think it's ridiculous. I'm sure that even now you are constraining yourself to show no emotion, although everything in you wants to jerk away from my touch. Do I repel you in some way, Fabia? Is that it?'

'Don't be——' She stopped abruptly at the fiery gleam that flashed for a second in the gold eyes. 'You're nothing to me. I don't know you, do I, so how could you repel me?' Repel? That would have been almost funny in other circumstances. She breathed a quick prayer of thanks that they were not alone, that there were other people near by. There was a sensual charm, a fascination, that pulled her in spite of herself, and she willed herself not to show it.

'You're very beautiful, Fabia.' His voice was like velvet now. 'But I suppose you're tired of hearing men say that.' His fingers left her hair and moved to her cheek, slowly wandering down her face to trace the outline of her mouth and then continuing to the hollow of her throat where a tiny pulse was beating madly.

'Don't ...' She sat as though turned to stone, her eyes brilliant in the stillness of her face.

'That's twice you've said that in as many minutes.' He smiled slowly. 'It's very ... challenging.' He bent forward and lightly kissed her lips before settling back into his seat again, his face wry. 'Something tells me I shall have to dig deep before I get to the bottom of this particular Southern belle.'

She didn't know how to reply and so she said nothing, taking a sip of the ice-cold water before raising her face to his again. 'What is it you want to say to me, anyway? I want to know,' she said determinedly, her eyes wary.

'I need your help,' he said softly, his eyes narrowing as they watched her start of surprise.

'My help?' She realised her voice was too shrill and lowered it quickly as her face turned scarlet. 'Mr—Alex, I'm sure there's nothing I can do to help you; if anyone is in control, you are!' There was a bite in the last words.

'You don't know what it is yet,' he said quietly. 'Didn't your mother ever tell you to look before you leap?'

'I've no intention of leaping anywhere,' she answered quickly, 'and I never had a mother, well, only in the biological sense, of course.' Why reveal that to him? she asked herself crossly.

She sensed a stiffening in the big body but his face was cool and remote when she glanced up, his expression unfathomable. 'Meaning?'

'I was an abandoned baby,' she said lightly, forcing an airy note into her voice. 'You know, "the police need to contact the mother at once as they fear she is in need of urgent medical attention" and all that.' She waited for him to speak, to express the usual surface sympathy, but when he said nothing she continued slowly. 'I was in a children's home until I was two and then a succession of foster homes until I was sixteen. Took my A levels when I was eighteen—that's how I met Joanie— and then out into the big world to earn my living. End of story.'

'I see.' He hadn't moved. 'So we've both been orphans all our lives in a way.'

'I hardly think our two situations were similar.' She smiled as she spoke but his face was straight as he looked hard at her.

'No?' He sighed softly as he leant back in his chair again. 'A lonely child is still a lonely child whether it has ten pence or ten pounds.'

'Or ten million?' Her voice was without humour. He didn't reply, just continuing to stare straight at her, and she flushed again as she realised the presumption of her words. 'I'm sorry, I shouldn't have said that,' she said quickly. 'I have no right to judge——'

'Well, it hasn't stopped you this far, so please don't change the habit of a lifetime just for me.' He was angry, very angry, she could feel it in the throb of his voice although his face was quite bland. She was beginning to realise that he gave little away, either in facial expression or body language, and that didn't fit into the mental picture she had of him at all. Playboy, socialite... She hadn't made a mistake, had she? An overwhelmingly catastrophic mistake?

'Do you work?' It came out quite baldly because she didn't stop to think, and she saw his surprise in the widening of those tawny-gold eyes seconds before the thick brown lashes came down to shield his face. There was silence for a moment.

'Yes, I do work, Fabia.' He glanced up again and now the careful mask was back in place. 'I have a large and very demanding business empire to manipulate with countless jobs and livelihoods hanging on the right decisions at the right time. But that isn't good news.' He smiled cynically. 'The latest social gathering I attend or the linking of my name with such and such an actress— now that——' he paused as his eyes sharpened '—that is good journalism.'

'Yes...' She looked up with immense relief as Xavier appeared at their side again to take their order. She would never have dreamt a few minutes before that she would actually be pleased to see the dapper little man, but now she gave him such a beaming smile that he was clearly quite taken aback. She felt at a complete and utter loss. All the preconceived ideas she had held about Alexander Cade seemed to be falling by the wayside and yet she didn't trust him. She looked at him from under her long silky lashes as he gave Xavier their order in fluent French. No, she didn't trust him an inch. He was too handsome, too rich, too powerful, a sight too much of everything, she reflected wryly. And what could a man like him possibly want with her? Fabia had no false modesty; she had been forced to evaluate herself from an early age and draw on any assets she had to the best of her ability.

True, she thought carefully, she was physically attractive and reasonably bright, but so were half the girls in London. In the world in which he moved beautiful people were ten a penny, so why had he taken the trouble to find her if not to punish her for the trick she had played on him and the financial loss it had caused? Panic became uppermost again and as her heart began to pound she took a hasty sip of water, holding the glass carefully in hands that trembled slightly. His power was frightening.

'There is no need to be frightened of me.' The golden-brown eyes were trained on her face again. 'I won't hurt you.'

'I'm not frightened of you,' she lied firmly with an upward tilt to her small chin. 'I don't frighten easily.'

'Better and better,' he drawled sardonically, and although he appeared to have taken her words at face value she had the uneasy feeling that the sharp cat gaze was alarmingly perceptive. She had been foolish, very foolish, to tangle with him, she thought tensely, and in spite of all his reassurances she felt instinctively that she was going to have to pay for her mistake. The debonair, rakish philanderer had been a mirage and instead she had been left facing a prowling lion, and indeed the simile seemed more than apt as she glanced at his mane of dark tawny-brown hair and the curiously gold eyes with their thick lashes that could be as clear and transparent as those of the king of the great cats, and just as unreadable. There was something about him, a hard brooding ruthlessness; he would fit into the inhospitable, cruel plains of Africa beautifully, stalking his prey carefully under a fierce burning sun and then just at the right moment——

'Your salmon soufflé, miss.' As the young waiter placed the glass bowl in front of her she almost jumped out of her skin, hiding her embarrassment with a cool smile as he disappeared again after placing Alex's dish in front of him.

'I was dreaming,' she said lightly to the attentive gaze.

'Really?' he said quietly, his voice smooth. 'I don't normally have my lady companions going off into a world of their own, but there have been several firsts with you, Fabia, in our somewhat short acquaintance. I have the distinct impression that life round you is never dull.'

There was no answer to that one and she didn't attempt to find one, suddenly finding that in spite of the enormous butterflies that were racing around her stomach she was really quite hungry. Lunch had been hours ago and had consisted of a snatched sandwich and paper cup of tepid coffee due to one of the ceaseless panics that cropped up every few days in the advertising world. She dipped a fork into the light, fluffy soufflé.

She didn't know what he was paying for the meal but whatever it was it was worth every penny, she reflected wryly as she tucked into the main course of trout, cooked in a wonderful concoction of orange liqueur and lemon, with baby new potatoes and fresh green beans and carrots. 'This is gorgeous...' She looked up as she spoke to find his amused gaze stroking her face, a sensuality in his eyes that caused her heart to pound.

'I'm glad you're enjoying it.' He let his glance wander for a moment down her slim shape. 'I didn't know if you were on a strict diet to keep that figure so perfect.'

'No fear.' Keep it friendly and general, Fabia, she thought silently, and you might just get away with this fiasco with nothing more alarming than an over-full stomach! Don't let him see how he affects you. 'I don't have weight problems; I suppose my job helps.'

'Really?' He leant forward slightly, amusement pulling at the firm mouth. 'Don't tell me you're a PE teacher or weight-lifter or some such thing?' His eyes were wicked.

'No.' For some reason she didn't want to tell him anything more about herself—she had regretted the earlier revelation as soon as it had slipped out—but there was no way she could not do so without appearing churlish. 'I work in advertising actually—nothing physical, except that we seem to race about from morning to dusk in a state of panic most days. If I remember to eat, which isn't often, I should think I've burned it all off again within minutes!' She smiled dismissively.

'I see.' His voice was casual but she had the feeling that every little thing she told him was being computed into an extensive memory bank and filed for future reference. She could believe now he managed a billion-turnover business. There was something very intimidating about this man, a sharp directness, an astuteness that lit the cold, handsome face from within. He was like a chameleon, she thought suddenly, able to change from one facet of his complicated personality to another at the blink of an eyelid. Tonight there had just been glimpses of the socialite flirt, but it was a mask that could instantly be brought out and donned in a second. Why hadn't she realised she had grabbed a tiger by the tail? Because he had fooled her as he fooled most people, she suspected, and he wanted it that way.

She glanced at him from under her lashes as she ate. He would be a dangerous adversary to contend with and hopefully she wouldn't have to, but if necessary... Her thoughts raced as her stomach filled. If necessary she would fight him. He might not be quite like Robin but he *had* been used to money and power all his life, and no doubt he thought he could acquire anything and anyone. But not this girl! Oh, no, not this girl.

'Dessert?' They had been sitting in silence sipping the excellent white wine he had ordered for some moments and as the waiter came to clear their plates Alex smiled at the shake of her head. 'Oh, come on, there must still be a little hole waiting to be filled.' He turned to the attentive waiter easily. 'Two helpings of that delicious berry trifle gâteau your chef does so marvellously.'

'Yes, Mr Cade.'

When they were alone again she glared at him across the small space, her eyes flashing blue sparks. 'Are you always so dictatorial?' she said sharply. 'Don't you listen to other people at all?' She suddenly felt trapped and overwhelmingly intimidated by the sheer presence of the man and it wasn't pleasant.

'I apologise,' he said calmly as the beautiful eyes turned icy, and she felt a little shiver snake down her back. Why didn't she just keep quiet, why antagonise him further? But she just couldn't help herself. It wasn't the dessert that had fired her but his dominant masculinity, which reached out to subdue her in a hundred and one ways.

She stared at him silently. She was behaving very badly and she didn't like herself this way but she disliked still more the strange melting feeling he could produce in her if they weren't fighting. 'I'm sorry,' she said tightly as she lowered her eyes to the wine glass in her hand. 'I'm on edge and as I said before, I don't think I can help you with anything, Mr Cade. I didn't want to come here and now I'm feeling——'

'Manoeuvred?' The cool sardonic voice brought her eyes shooting up to his. 'But you *are* being manoeuvred, my dear Fabia, and the name is Alex, remember?' He smiled slowly. 'I think you are honest enough to recognise that you owe me, yes?' She stared at him blankly as her heart began to pound. 'Yes?' His voice was cruelly insistent.

'But——' Her protest was cut off by the arrival of the berry trifle gâteau, and as the waiter placed the mouth-watering slice of soft cake running with brandy, whipped cream and ripe sugared berries in front of her Alex caught her eye, his expression enigmatic.

'Eat and enjoy.' His tone was uncompromising and she suddenly realised that what she did or did not eat would have very little bearing on the outcome of this disastrous evening. He had brought her out to be alone with her and for a purpose that had yet to be made clear. It could be he was just like all the other men she seemed to come into contact with these days, one thing on their minds and one thing only. But she doubted it. She looked again at the hard, handsome face. No, it wasn't as simple as that with him. He could have any girl he wanted. He didn't need to coerce a reluctant woman into his bed. Then what on earth *was* it? She gave up for the moment, picked up her spoon and dug into the rich sweet mixture with a guilty feeling of pleasure, secretly pleased that in this instance he had won the battle, and then instantly disgusted with herself.

'Now.' As she poured a liberal helping of cream into the dark aromatic depths of her coffee he finally spoke, and in spite of the portent of what was to come she felt a sense of relief. His silence over the last few minutes had been a little unnerving and she had known instinctively that he was collecting his thoughts in order to make plain to her what the evening had been about. 'I have a proposal to put to you which I want you to consider carefully over the next day or two, after which time I shall be in contact with you for your decision.' He cleared his throat.

'Yes?' He was speaking as though he were in the boardroom but the controlled, distant voice had a calming effect on the fluttering in her stomach until the tawny eyes fixed her again.

'I am in need of some assistance in a somewhat...delicate area and I would be grateful if you would listen quietly to what I have to say until I have finished. Do you understand?'

She nodded slowly, quelling the spurt of anger the formal, authoritative voice had caused. He was an enigma, this Alexander Cade, she thought silently as she looked into the stiff restrained face. Definitely an enigma.

'As I mentioned to you earlier, I was brought up by my paternal grandmother on her estate in Cumbria until school age, after which time I divided my life between boarding-school and her home in the holidays. She took the place of mother and father in my life and did it very well considering that when I was first foisted on her she was already in her early fifties.'

'I don't see——'

He cut her voice off abruptly, his face darkening. 'Please be quiet, Fabia, and let me get on with it.' Just for a fleeting moment she had the impression he was finding this difficult, but then she dismissed the thought as fanciful.

'My grandmother is eighty-seven and has been in poor health the last six months. I have had a word with her consultant and she isn't expected to live beyond a few months. Her heart is very tired.' He looked at her intently. 'I care very much for my grandmother, Fabia.'

'Yes, well, that's only natural...' She had no idea where this strange conversation was leading but a little trickle of apprehension was running down her spine at the determined expression in the beautiful gold eyes watching her so closely.

'She is a rather... forceful old lady who speaks her mind with less tact than is comfortable at times.' A slight smile touched the hard mouth. 'You would have a lot in common with her, I think. However——' he raised his hand quickly as she opened her mouth to speak '—that is by the by. As you have already pointed out, repeatedly, my name has often been linked with various young ladies who have come and gone through the years, some of which I have introduced to my grandmother and some not. It would give her a great deal of pleasure if she thought that I had a... particular friend at the moment. She is a born matchmaker, probably due to having an Italian mother herself—who knows?'

She was staring at him very hard now with a faintly incredulous expression turning her large eyes navy blue. He couldn't be suggesting...? No, it was ridiculous. She had misunderstood him.

'As I said, time is short. I would like her last Christmas to be a happy one with the feeling that everything is right in her small world. Do you understand what I mean, Fabia?'

She shook her head dazedly. 'There are several women I could take home to meet her but none of them would appeal to her and *all* of them would present me with interminable problems once the festive season is over. I have neither the time nor the inclination for such complications at the moment. I am in the middle of several important business transactions and can't waste time on trivia.' He was still speaking in the distant, unemotional tone he had used throughout, which made the whole thing even more preposterous. He couldn't mean——

'I need a nice steady two-feet-on-the-ground girl who knows exactly where she stands with me long-term but is confident enough to charm my grandmother into thinking that maybe, just maybe, this is the one for her grandson. No lies, no promises; I shall take you there as merely a friend but I know my grandmother—she will immediately plan for all sorts of possibilities, and for once I shall let her.'

'Take me...?' Her voice was a breathless squeak and now the full barrage of that tawny feline gaze was trained on her and his voice was anything but impassive as he leant forward until he was just a breath away, his eyes liquid gold.

'Yes, you, my golden-haired little beauty,' he said softly. 'In spite of looking like the fairy on top of the Christmas tree you have more guts than most men I know. Anyone who can make the sort of escape you did from that washroom in full evening dress after plucking a man back from the jaws of death and putting on a great show for me all night will find a piece of harmless deception child's play. I want you to accompany me to my grandmother's home for Christmas, Fabia Grant, as my girlfriend. Now, finish your coffee and don't say a word for at least five minutes.'

CHAPTER THREE

'YOU can't be serious!' Fabia didn't wait five seconds to explode, let alone five minutes. 'I've never heard of such a crazy idea in my life!'

'Crazy? Why crazy?' There was a softness to the deep voice that spoke of molten steel but she was too incensed to notice.

'Me, accompany you, to goodness knows where and as your girlfriend? You must think I was born yesterday! I suppose this charade would involve us sharing the same room and so on? All friends together?' She glared at him furiously. 'At the risk of repeating an old cliché, Mr Alexander Cade, I'm not that sort of girl.' Sheer anger had quelled the trembling in her stomach.

'I'm fully aware what sort of girl you are,' he said icily, 'which is why I have made the suggestion in the first place. I don't mince words when I'm setting up a business deal, Fabia. All the facts are out in the open and there are no hidden "punches" involved. I don't know what sort of men you are used to dealing with but don't make the mistake of putting me in that catagory! This would be an arrangement between the two of us, in writing if you like, for a specified amount of time and with a set fee of your choosing. You would sleep alone. I would sleep alone. Got it?'

'Now look——'

He brought her indignant voice to an abrupt halt. 'And I have made it perfectly clear exactly where we are going. Cumbria. You have heard of that part of the country, I take it?' he asked derisively.

'Of course I have,' she hissed angrily. 'But this whole idea is preposterous. I *can't* believe you're serious.'

'Of course I am serious,' he returned coldly, 'and there is nothing preposterous whatsoever in what I am suggesting. I need a service which you may or may not be able to supply... Have you already made arrangements for the Christmas period?' he asked suddenly, his eyes narrowing on the heavy blonde hair and fragile face. 'I am quite prepared to pay for any cancellations. Or to soothe any irate boyfriend...?' His voice hardened slightly.

There was a question in the last words which she chose to ignore. 'My plans are my own affair,' she said sharply, her eyes glittering angrily as he leant forward to take her left hand in his.

'Of course they are,' he agreed smoothly. 'However, I think we have ascertained that there is no immediate family to complicate matters, and you aren't wearing a ring on the third finger of your left hand, so I assume the boyfriend, if there is one, is not serious?' The feel of his warm flesh on hers was curling her toes. The question was there again and she was furious at his autocratic assumption that he had the right to interrogate her about the state of her love-life, and even more furious at the effect his touch was having.

'You really have got a cheek,' she spat angrily, jerking her hand away so violently that it hit the table with a dull thud. 'I don't even know how to play your girlfriend! We are worlds apart, as you very well know. Take this restaurant, for instance——'

'Yes?' He leant forward, his face intent.

'It's just so...plush, so removed from anything I would normally go to. You eat at this sort of place all the time, don't you?' she finished accusingly.

'And that is the main cause of your concern about my proposal? That we eat at different restaurants?' His

voice was mocking and cool and in that moment she felt
a stab of sheer hate pierce her as she looked into the
narrowed amber eyes. He thought he only had to say
the word and things would fall magically into place. Well,
perhaps that happened if you were rich enough to buy
and sell half of London, but everyone had to be dis-
appointed some time! Her thoughts were mirrored in the
clear blue of her eyes and as he kept his gaze fixed on
her face he smiled slowly, his face unreadable.

'I told you I wouldn't accept any decision tonight,' he
said blandly after a full minute of tense silence had
ensued. 'I will contact you in forty-eight hours when
you have had time to consider my suggestion properly.'
He settled back in his chair.

'Oh, it is a suggestion, then?' she said bitingly. 'For
a minute there I thought it was an order.'

'Not at all,' he said calmly. 'However, a few things I
would just reiterate. First, you do owe me, Fabia,
whether you care to admit it or not, and this would be
a perfect way to cancel your debt—and, believe me, it's
quite a large one.'

'I don't have a debt,' she began furiously, but he held
up his hand for silence and something in the hard,
handsome face made her bite her lip as her voice faltered
away.

'Secondly, I am in something of a fix for the reasons
I have explained. I need to approach this situation as a
business deal, something separate from my private life,
you understand?' She glared at him silently. 'And the
point that you are not used to my kind of lifestyle is
quite unimportant. If you accept this offer you are at
liberty to just be yourself; I would expect nothing more.
The only thing I would ask you to do is to force some
degree of warmth into our relationship.' He smiled at
her angry face. 'Only when we are in company, of course.

In private you could be your normal waspish little self shrinking from my touch like the original shy violet.'

What she would give to slap that mocking smirk off his handsome face! She schooled her features into a cool mask with considerable effort.

'And if I did agree to this mad idea—not that I would do, of course,' she added coldly, 'how do you explain to your grandmother that we met? What am I supposed to be, one of your employees who caught the boss's eye or a modern-day Cinderella taken out of the gutter by a passing noble?'

'You really must try to curb this enormous inferiority complex, Fabia,' he said smoothly. 'Maybe a course of psychoanalysis would help. You are just as good as me, my dear.'

'*I* know that!' she snarled ferociously, eyeing him with angry antagonism as he began to shake with silent laughter, his eyes aglow. 'And you haven't answered my question.'

'Why, I would just tell it as it is,' he replied after a few moments when he could restrain his amusement. 'I don't suppose for a moment you and your friend were the original recipients of those tickets. What was it, a last-minute gift?' She nodded slowly. 'There you are, then, that's all anyone needs to know. I met you there for the first time, our eyes met across a crowded room and from that point the rest of the world faded into oblivion.' There was a strange note in his voice that she couldn't place and she stared at him hard. 'Simple, eh?'

'I'm not doing this, Mr Cade,' she said flatly.

'It's Alex!' This time the voice was stone-cold and his face was grim. 'And I've told you, I won't accept any decision now. I will contact you as arranged. Now, have you finished?' He raised a hand and immediately the waiter was at their side with their coats.

'Don't you pay?' she asked in amazement as he escorted her from the restaurant with a firm hand under her elbow, to the smiles and nods of most people present.

'I have an account here which is settled monthly,' he answered quietly, his face hardening at her satisfied little nod. 'And don't start that "we're so different" rubbish again,' he warned coldly as they stepped on to the icy pavement.

'Well, it's true,' she protested as the Bentley glided to a halt in front of them as though by magic. 'You must see it.'

'Are you seriously telling me that you don't believe two people from different backgrounds can meet and fall in love and live together happily all their lives?' His eyes were piercing her as she sat uncomfortably in the warm lush interior of the car. 'Is that what you're saying?' He was uncomfortably close.

'Of course not.' She flushed hotly. 'But it's rare. It can happen, but it's rare. And that isn't what we're talking about. We are discussing persuading your grandmother that you find me attractive.' Did he *have* to be so darned good-looking?

'And what's so strange about that?' he asked carefully.

'With all the women you've——' she nearly said 'had' and altered it quickly '—known? They're beautiful and famous and——'

'Boring,' he finished quietly. 'Not all, I admit, but a surfeit of rich goodies becomes unpalatable after a time.'

'You didn't find that meal tonight unpalatable,' she said quickly, deliberately misunderstanding him. There was a stillness in his profile that unnerved her a little although she didn't know why, but she disliked the way this conversation was heading.

'No, the meal tonight was wonderful,' he agreed quietly, turning to look at her for just a fleeting second.

As his eyes met hers in the shadowed darkness of the car she felt something akin to an electric shock shoot down her spine and drew back sharply into her seat, her eyes widening in unspoken protest. It was as though he was making love to her, without touching her, without even speaking. He was dangerous! Dangerous and seductive and compelling. He held her glance for a long moment before turning to look out of the window at the brightly lit busy London street, full of small wine bars, tiny restaurants and the odd fish and chip shop incongruous against its upper-class neighbours. 'Of course the salad at that particular restaurant is delicious,' he said blandly as the car sped smoothly along. 'I often have that along with a chop or seafood.' The mind-stunning moment passed but the vibrations were still with Fabia when the car drew up outside the dismal block of flats, and she stiffened as he left the car and opened the door for her, helping her out with old-fashioned courtesy, his face inscrutable.

'Thank you for the meal; it was lovely,' she said hurriedly as she stepped on to the uneven paving slabs that led over to the big glass doors of the silent building, holding out her hand dismissively. 'Goodnight, Alex.'

'I'll see you to the door,' he said quietly, his eyes travelling over her flushed cheeks and coming to rest on the wide full mouth. 'Just to the door.' He looked down at her silently.

'There's no need . . .' Her voice died away as he took her arm again, his hand firm. She was wearing three-inch heels but in spite of that he still towered over her by a good four inches, and she found it peculiarly gratifying to be in the company of a man who was a good deal taller than herself for once. At five feet nine inches plus heels she normally found that she was on a level with most men, a fact which in the past had not bothered her at all. Nevertheless, his height was . . . satisfying. She caught the thought and brought it severely to heel. There was nothing about him she liked! Nothing!

As the old grimy lift took them jerkily upwards she glanced at him from the corner of her eye. I wonder what he's thinking? she thought curiously. This grubby, somewhat seedy part of London had been the best that she could afford in the early days, and as she had progressed in her career she had found herself loath to move from the cosy little flat, having renovated it with loving care and a good deal of elbow grease. It was bright and clean and unusual, a reflection of the complicated personality who lived within its walls, each room alive with colour and comfort.

As the lift shuddered to a halt on her floor and the faded yellow doors slowly opened she stuck out her hand again. 'We've arrived,' she said brightly. 'Thank you again.'

'I said to the door,' he returned coolly, stepping out of the metal box with her and walking along the corridor that always seemed to smell slightly of cooked cabbage. 'Safely home?' He leaned against the wall as she hunted in her handbag for her key, annoyed to find herself all fingers and thumbs as he stared at her, his expression sardonic and his powerful body relaxed. 'Against all the odds?'

'Not at all.' She smiled cautiously. A few more seconds and she was home and dry. As she retrieved her key from the muddle at the bottom of her handbag he stepped forward suddenly, taking her completely by surprise.

'I'm probably going to regret this in view of the fact that I shall be completely blotting my copybook as far as you are concerned,' he said huskily, pulling her in his arms and taking her mouth in a long, hard kiss as he moved her round so that her back was against the wall and his body pressing against hers. For a moment she was too stunned to react and then, as the kiss deepened into a seductively sensual caress and she felt the length of his hard body moulded intimately against hers, she realised, with a shock of horror, that part of her had been waiting for this, hoping for it.

The expensively delicious smell of him was intoxicating, surrounding her with an undeniable aura of masculinity that both thrilled and repelled her, repelled because she must remember, *she had to remember*, that she was just one of many, a trinket to play with for a time and then thrown away without a moment's thought. A rich man's toy!

Hadn't that agonising time with Robin taught her anything? Was she completely crazy? As the condemning thoughts hit her mind like a deluge of cold water she froze in his arms and he immediately sensed it, moving away as he ran a hand through the dark brown hair, his eyes rueful. 'Stupid, Alex, my boy, real stupid...' He was muttering as though to himself and the next instant, without a word of goodbye, he was walking away towards the waiting lift, entering its doors without a backward glance, his walk easy and free like a big relaxed cat.

She stood for a moment as though transfixed to the spot, listening to the sounds of the ancient machinery grinding downwards, her thoughts in turmoil and her body on fire. There was an ache in her body that was almost painful, each nerve-ending vitally alive and seeking relief. What was the matter with her? What *was* the matter? She almost stamped her foot in impotent rage and disgust at her weakness and heard the phone ringing in her flat with a mixture of irritation and relief. It would be Joanie, no doubt. 'Hi, it's me,' Joanie said breathlessly. 'Well, what's happened? Are you all right? Did it go well? What did he say?'

'It's OK, it's OK, no problem,' Fabia said reassuringly, but the words sounded hollow even to herself. 'I'm shattered though, Joanie. Can we talk in the morning?'

'But what did he want?' Joanie persisted doggedly.

'Suffice to say the ball's well and truly in my court and I'm not starting to play, but as I said I'll explain in the morning. Night, Joanie.' She couldn't make small talk, she just couldn't!

She put down the receiver on further protestations and after collapsing in a heap on the bed flailed herself yet again.

Why had she ever agreed to go with Joanie to that ill-fated function in the first place and, once there, what on earth had possessed her to act in such a way? She lay back on the bed as her thoughts raced. She knew why. Everything had so resembled the first time she had met Robin and she had rebelled, hotly and violently, against ever being put in the same position again.

The thoughts that she had kept back for months surfaced in excruciating clearness and she was too exhausted to fight them, giving in to their agony as she went back in time to that night, seven years ago, when she had been eighteen and thought the world was out there just for her.

She had been wearing red, she remembered tiredly, a red velvet evening dress that had moulded itself to her figure like a second skin, sleeveless, backless and incredibly daring. It had been hired specially for the great night; it wasn't often a working girl like her won tickets for a ball that people would kill for, and the women in the shop had urged her to take that particular dress in preference to the one she had chosen, a more subdued little number in pale green.

She had only been in London four weeks and living in digs at the time, at a loss to understand the great city or its people, nervous, excited and wonderfully aware

that every man's eyes were being drawn to her that night,
picking her out from the three other girls she had gone
with in a manner that brought a flush to her cheeks and
glitter to her eyes.

Robin had noticed her in the first five minutes, appearing at her side with two glasses of champagne, his
light blue eyes frankly appreciative and his smooth,
almost white blond hair and unusual good looks bowling
her over. He had turned on the charm and she had been
lost, a little girl alone in the big city and the perfect
pushover, she thought bitterly, her mouth hardening.

Robin had been clever, she had to give him that. So
caring, so gentle, so considerate at first. And then...
'If you love me you'll want us to be as one, darling,' he
had murmured night after night as they had kissed and
fondled in his magnificently luxurious apartment or in
the back of his white Rolls-Royce. 'I love you so much,
I want to know everything about you.' He had wined
and dined her, taking her to the best restaurants, the
most exciting shows, dazzling and bewitching her,
picking her up from work now and again, insisting that
nothing was too much trouble for his 'darling'.

She had realised later, when it was far, far too late,
that he had used his limitless wealth and influence like
a drug, increasing the dosage little by little until she was
completely hooked. It hadn't mattered that he was twenty
years older than her at the time. 'Age means nothing to
us, sweetheart,' he had assured her over and over again
and, loving him as she did, trusting him implicitly, unable
to believe her luck that this caring, handsome, tender
man actually loved her, she had agreed wholeheartedly.
Indeed there were times when, exhausted from a grinding
day at the office, the very bottom rung in a massively
tall ladder, she had felt years older than him.

He had assured her that the playboy image, the fact
that he lived on the vast wealth he had inherited from

his father without ever dirtying a finger in work, was all a figment of people's imagination, and although, secretly, she had wondered at times, she had accepted that along with all the other lies.

Three months after they had met, when he'd considered she was ripe, he had issued an ultimatum, his eyes full of pain and his face woebegone. 'If you love me, darling, really love me, you can't let anything separate us,' he had said mournfully, shaking his head gently. 'This is killing me, to love you, to hold you in my arms and then have you draw back at the last moment. I can't take any more, Fabia. It has to be all or nothing.' He had ridiculed her idea of keeping herself chaste until she was married. 'We don't need to wait for that, darling. You know I love you, that I'll always love you.' And she had believed him. Utterly, completely. It had been so wonderful to have someone tell her that she mattered after the long years of being moved from one home to another, never really belonging, never knowing if she dared presume to put down tentative roots.

And so she had promised him. That weekend she would come to him. In his flat. She would stay the weekend, cook and care for him, and love him as he asked. Be everything he wanted.

'Stupid, stupid, stupid...' She groaned at the memory, rolling over into a tight little ball and putting her hands over her ears as though she could shut out the sounds of that woman's screaming when she had discovered her and Robin in the huge bed with black silk sheets. And Robin's rage. Rage that his mistress had come back from her trip to Paris too soon. Rage that he hadn't consummated his affair with Fabia. Rage that he had been found out. Rage that his careful manipulating had gone wrong.

'No more.' She rose, pale and shaking, from the bed and, after stripping off her clothes, padded into the bathroom, standing under the hot shower with her head raised to the water and letting the cleansing flow wash over her until it turned cool. A twenty-five-year-old virgin in London. She smiled to herself soberly. There were probably more about than met the eye. She wasn't unique.

Something had died in her that night. The humiliation and the aftermath had hurt too deeply, destroyed too many childish dreams of a knight on a white charger, for her ever to be the same again. She had lost all her self-respect for a long, long time but she had regained it now and nobody, *nobody*, would ever take it away again. She had had the odd boyfriend after a time but none of them had remotely stirred her dead heart. She viewed the whole male sex without rose-coloured glasses, seeing them as vain, selfish and shallow most of the time with the odd exception here and there proving the rule. And she *would not* be fooled again! Not by a tawny-eyed giant with a glib line in persuasion whose kisses were out of this world. She caught herself with a sense of shock. She didn't need kisses and she didn't need any complications in her life! She was a career girl who had got everything very nicely under control, thank you, and if, occasionally, in the dark of the night when sleep was a million miles away, she yearned for a different life, the cold harsh light of day soon put her to rights. White knights and white weddings were in story-books.

A pale watery dawn was creeping into the small bedroom when at last her eyelids closed in sleep, and she slept soundly and deeply until the shrill ring of the doorbell brought her jerking awake.

It had to be Brian, she thought furiously as she stumbled to the door, pulling a robe over the blue silk pyjamas she was wearing. Only Brian would be inconsiderate enough to ring the bell at eight o'clock on a Saturday morning.

'Just returning the coffee.' Brian's face was a picture of innocence. 'Didn't get you up, did I?'

'Yes!' She was too tired to be polite, reaching out for the coffee jar as she spoke.

'Sorry.' He didn't look it. 'Who was that guy I saw you with last night? New boyfriend?'

His tone was distinctly hostile and brought her fully awake with a little thud. What now? She really didn't need this on top of everything else. 'I think that's my business, Brian, don't you?' She made no effort to soften her words. 'Now I'd really like to get back to bed if you don't mind.'

'Don't mind at all.' He had pushed past her into the flat before she was aware of it and walked into the small lounge with swaggering steps. 'Busy night, was it? Strenuous?' His meaning was unmistakable, as was the leer on his face, and for a second she felt a stab of fear before hot anger rose to take its place.

'Get out of my flat, Brian,' she said coldly. 'I don't remember inviting you in.'

'You never do, do you?' he said softly, his thick lips wet as the small eyes ran over her body. 'Got to have a Bentley or something first, eh? Like lover-boy?'

'You followed us out into the street?' The windows were on the other side of the flats so he couldn't have seen Alex's car from there. 'Just who do you think you are?'

'Someone who can give you a good time if you'd let me.' He took a step towards her. 'How about it?'

'I suggest you leave now, Brian.' She stood her ground and he shambled to a halt, picking nervously at his nails as he faced her.

'Why?' Again she felt that stab of fear but kept her voice cool and firm as she spoke.

'Because my new boyfriend would be most upset to find you bothering me and, as you can imagine, he is rich enough to buy and sell you ten times over. He could make things very unpleasant for you, believe me; he knows people.'

'Oh, yeah?' The threat had worked, it was there in the reddening of his plump face.

'Yes.' She looked at him hard.

'You mean you're seeing him again?' he said slowly.

'Yes, I am,' she said quickly, too quickly; he caught the inflexion in her voice as she spoke the lie.

'I don't believe you.' He looked at her hard. 'Men like him don't bother with the likes of you once they've had their fun.' She agreed perfectly with the sentiment but wasn't about to let him know that.

'As it happens I'm spending Christmas with him, OK?' she said firmly. 'And please get out, Brian, I'm getting cold standing here talking to you.' The ease with which the lie had fallen from her lips plus her matter-of-fact tone seemed to defuse the situation and he glanced at her again before walking slowly to the open door.

'Huh!' What exactly the exclamation was meant to express she didn't know and didn't care as she shut the door quickly, sliding the bolt in place for extra comfort.

What a creep! She found she was shaking slightly as she ran a shower, sleep being a million miles away now. The warm water did a lot to calm her and as she dressed slowly she began to berate herself for being panicked into telling such a ridiculous story. She wasn't going anywhere with anyone—especially not Alexander Cade. Still, no one would be any the wiser, she thought comfortably after a time as she made herself tea and toast, and it had served a purpose. She had been looking for a way to get through to Brian for weeks and it looked as though it had been dropped in her lap. She ought to be grateful to Alex really.

She spent a lazy day at home doing a hundred and one jobs she had been putting off for weeks, ringing

Joanie in the evening and putting her mind at rest before falling into bed at the ridiculously early time of nine o'clock, tired out.

She had been invited to spend the Sunday with a married colleague from work whose husband was in Saudi Arabia and meet her children, and she was glad now that she had accepted. They had a wonderful day, lighting a bonfire in the garden in the afternoon after a huge dinner of roast beef and Yorkshire pudding and then taking the family dog, a comical little mongrel called Rambo—'You'd know why if you lived with him,' her friend said wryly—to Hyde Park for a long walk before muffins and tea in front of the fire.

She arrived home late, tired but glowing from a day in the fresh air, to find Alex leaning lazily against the door of her flat as she stepped out of the lift.

'Good evening, Fabia.' His voice stopped her in her tracks and as she met the cool gold eyes she was aware of Brian's door being slightly ajar. 'I've just been having a little chat with your neighbour. Seedy individual, isn't he?' The door closed with a definite click and she glanced at Alex's face to see he was smiling wryly. 'I've warned him off in no uncertain terms. I'm afraid he won't dare speak to you again. Right or wrong?'

'Dead right and long overdue.' She looked at him carefully. 'What has he been saying?'

'I've no intention of having a conversation in the middle of this corridor,' he said coolly. 'Shall we...?' He indicated her front door with a wave of his hand and she had no choice but to step past him and unlock it. 'Now...' He looked at her tightly as she shut the front door. 'I understand I shall have the pleasure of your company at Christmas? A delightful prospect.' His eyes were speculative as they met her shocked blue gaze, narrowing slightly in silent enquiry at the stunned expression on her face. 'That *is* what you told love's young dream next door?' She had forgotten how devastatingly handsome he was.

'Yes, no; I didn't mean...' Her voice trailed away helplessly. 'I just...' She stopped again.

'Yes?' She couldn't read anything from his bland face and as her mind searched for a way out of what had turned into a monstrous parody she finally decided she would have to tell him the truth. There was absolutely no way she was going to spend Christmas as his leading lady in some macabre play so the only alternative was to explain things properly and throw herself on his mercy. Mercy? She shut her eyes briefly and then took courage and glanced at him carefully under her eyelashes. He had been relatively reasonable up to now considering the circumstances of their first encounter, and he had left the choice of whether she accompany him to Cumbria or not up to her, so it should be all right. Shouldn't it?

Just for a moment, as she looked directly at him, there was something quite ruthless in the brilliant golden-brown eyes that made her shiver, but when she looked again his face appeared quite bland, even pleasant, and she gave herself a little admonitory shake. You're getting paranoid, she told herself firmly, and it's got to stop.

'Fabia? Shall we be seated?' He settled himself comfortably into an easy-chair as he spoke, crossing one leg over his knee as his hands stretched along the back of the chair. For some reason the action seemed intimidating, perhaps because it highlighted the strong muscular shoulders, broad chest and long powerful legs. She gulped silently.

She had never met a man whose masculinity was worn so powerfully before; it was almost tangible, virile and dangerous, and she didn't like the tremors that snaked down her spine, she didn't like them at all. She didn't want to respond to the message his body was sending to her femininity. He was the enemy—all his type were.

'Well?' he said softly when she still didn't speak. 'Let's have it.'

'What?' She stared at him in consternation. 'What do you mean?' Was he psychic as well?

'That's for you to tell me,' he said quietly. 'You've been like a cat on a hot tin roof since you came in. What's wrong?' He smiled slowly. 'Or is it my animal magnetism?'

'Alex...' She leant forward imploringly, her hair glowing like liquid gold in the shadowed room and her blue eyes enormous. 'It's all a mistake, about me coming to Cumbria with you, I mean. I never meant you to know, I only told Brian——' She paused helplessly. She wasn't making a very good job of this, she thought miserably, searching her mind for a way to explain things that wouldn't make a bad situation ten times worse.

'I think you'd better start at the beginning.' In her anxiety she didn't notice the coldness in his soft voice or the way the teasing glow had died from his eyes, leaving them two hard chips of yellow glass. 'Let's have it all.'

So she told him, stumbling a little and keeping her eyes on her hands clenched into fists and when at last she ground to a halt she waited a moment before raising her face to meet his gaze. What she saw there made her blood run cold. If she had thought he was angry that first night it was mere irritation compared to the black rage that had his whole body in a tight grip now. He was furiously, violently angry.

'You really are priceless.' The words were ground out slowly through gritted teeth, a savagery in his voice that made her breath catch nervously in her throat. 'An absolute twenty-four-carat winner.' She shrank back in her chair as he came to crouch over her, his face twisted into a black satanic mask and his eyes flashing fire. 'What do you think I am? First you attempt to make me the laughing-stock of London with that cute little trick you pulled, losing me a great deal of money in the process, and then you duck out and vanish into thin air, leaving me with the proverbial egg on my face! Not content with that you now propose to use me in some duplicitous plan of your own without even informing me I'm bailing you out. I can't believe you, I really can't believe what I've just heard.'

'I told you, Brian——'

'Forget Brian,' he snarled savagely. 'I've made it clear to that scum that you are strictly out of bounds. Just concentrate on me for now.' He straightened slowly, staring at her from eyes that were slanted into narrow gold slits. 'Brian is the least of your problems, angel-face, believe me.'

She remained frozen in her chair, her face upturned to his, hardly daring to breathe.

'No one has ever been foolish enough to treat me like this before and I'm going to make damn sure you never make that mistake again. I don't know what's gone on in your life and at this moment in time I don't care, but you are going to be brought to heel, my girl, severely to heel.'

'Alex——'

'Don't "Alex" me.' His voice was soft now with a quiet deadliness that chilled her blood. 'From now on we play the game my way, understand? I've tried the softly-softly approach but you don't understand normal reasonable behaviour, do you?' His eyes glittered furiously. 'No matter, angel-face, we'll communicate on your terms. You will come with me to my grandmother's home for Christmas whether it fits into your plans or not, and you will do *exactly* as I tell you. Is that clear?' His eyes raked her ferociously as he spoke.

'I will not!' She had been too stunned by his unexpected rage to react before but now an anger to match his had her in its grip. 'You can't make me! With all your money you can't make me!' She made to rise but he pushed her down violently.

'Don't make me show you what I can or can't do,' he said slowly, the authority in his voice intimidating her even as she tried to fight it. 'You'll regret it, bitterly, if you do. I won't be taken for a ride by you or anyone else.'

'I wasn't——'

Her voice strangled in her throat as he reached out a hand and grasped a handful of hair, drawing her up to him slowly. 'How can anyone who looks so... fragile be so hard?'

'I'm not hard!' Her body was pressed into his now and her head tilted to look up into his dark face.

'No?' His mouth twisted in the semblance of a smile. 'You mean there's another side I haven't been privileged enough to glimpse yet?' His fingers loosened in her hair, slowly moving across her head to the back of her neck as his breathing thickened. 'I don't know why the hell I'm bothering with you at all except that maybe I believe that other side is there after all.' She stood absolutely still, hardly daring to breathe. The look on his face and the stirring in the hard male body pressed against hers told her more clearly than words of his arousal and she had never felt more vulnerable in her life, more threatened. Not so much because of his rage or passion, she was honest enough to admit to herself, but more because she couldn't trust herself not to respond.

'Fabia...' Her name was a groan on his lips as he bent to nuzzle his face in the soft silk of her hair, his mouth moving to her ears and throat in soft feather-like kisses that brought an immediate hot ache trembling forth in her lower stomach, and as his mouth fastened on hers with a touch of violence in its intensity she found

herself straining to meet his need with her body even as
her mind told her this was madness.

'Why do you fight me when it could always be like
this?' His voice was so soft that she could barely hear
it and as she felt his fingers on the tiny pearl buttons of
her blouse she shut her eyes tightly. She had to stop this;
what was she doing . . . ?

'No, please, Alex . . .' Her voice was lost as he claimed
her mouth again, and as she felt her bra slip and his
fingers move to cup the silky fullness of her breasts a
piercingly sweet pleasure took over her senses at the same
time as a little cold voice hammered into her brain,
Again? You are inviting all this again? And with him?

'I said no!' As she wrenched herself backwards out
of his arms she pulled her blouse so violently across her
chest that she felt the thin material tear. 'Don't touch
me!'

'What the——?' As he saw the panic in her eyes his
hands, which had gone out to grasp her, froze in mid-
air, a stillness taking over his features as he turned away,
walking over to the other side of the room and standing
with his back bent and his hands resting palm down on
the small coffee-table as he struggled for control.

She sank down into the chair she had vacated, her
mind numbed and blank and her breath coming in little
panting sobs. They remained suspended in a frozen
tableau for a full minute and then he raised himself
slowly, turning and looking over to where she sat huddled
in the chair, his eyes as cold as ice.

'I don't know what all that was about, Fabia, but if
you thought you could twist your way out of doing what
I want you are dead wrong.' She stared at him silently,
her eyes huge in her white face. 'You owe me and you
are going to pay your debt. You'll come to Cumbria and
behave beautifully, not a foot—not a toe—out of place.
Do you understand?'

'I hate you.' As her whispered words reached him his face stiffened.

'Maybe.' His voice grew softer. 'But you're still coming. And afterwards I shall let you go, a few days older but a whole lot wiser.'

'You can't make me——'

'I can and I will, sweetheart.' He was calmer now but with a ruthless severity that was more chilling than his anger. 'I've given you every chance and you've blown it. Well, such is life.' He shook his head slowly as he walked to the door, his eyes resting on her face with a touch of biting contempt in their gold depths.

'I don't like to be played with, and, until you learn that, life is going to be very difficult.' He paused with his hand on the handle. 'And a word of warning: don't try and escape again, Fabia. The world isn't big enough to hide you. One of the advantages of having money is that it makes the world considerably smaller. I'll be in touch. Goodnight.'

It was a full minute before she could persuade her trembling legs to move after he had left, and then she stumbled over to the door, shooting the bolt into place with shaking hands and sinking down on to the carpet weakly.

He had trapped her! She groaned softly. Or maybe she had trapped herself? Why, oh, why had she told Brian she was spending Christmas with Alex? She could have handled Brian, but not this man. Not this man with his tawny cat-like eyes that could harden into stone and his limitless, terrifying wealth. He was too powerful to fight, with his sensual charm and compelling sexuality, and she seemed to have no defence against him. At the last thought she stiffened. No! He could *attempt* to subjugate her, impose his will over hers, but the final outcome would be up to her. She raised herself from the floor slowly. And, as sure as she drew breath, never,

never again in the whole of her life would she allow herself to be crushed and defeated, broken at the feet of some man. She would rather die first.

She straightened her slender shoulders for battle, her mouth set in grim determination. She would go with Alexander Cade to his grandmother's home and act the part that fate, and a big golden-eyed barbarian, had allotted to her to the best of her ability. She had no other choice. But if he thought he had won he was wrong! Her eyes narrowed ominously.

He would never reach the real Fabia Grant, never touch the woman who had been born that night seven years ago amid heartbreak, disillusion and bitter humiliation, never touch the core on which she had built a new life.

She simply wouldn't let him.

CHAPTER FOUR

'ARE you warm enough?' Fabia started violently as Alex's cool, quiet voice interrupted her thoughts.

'I'm fine, thank you,' she replied stiffly, and he nodded slowly with his eyes fixed on the road ahead, the windscreen wipers clearing the snow from the glass in steady monotonous rhythm. They had been driving for an hour and the snow was coming down thicker now, fat starry flakes patterning the cold glass for a split-second before the wipers cleared them relentlessly from view, the midday sky heavy and bleak.

She flexed her toes in the warmth from the car heater, reflecting silently that the smart high-heeled shoes that had seemed so appropriate in London were fast becoming most unsuitable in view of the worsening weather. The snow was already several inches thick and showed no signs of abating; in fact the thick grey sky promised much more. Still, it couldn't be helped. She glanced at Alex's severe profile from under her lashes, her stomach tightening as it dawned on her afresh that she was committed to this man's company for a whole week. Christmas had never arrived so quickly, she thought wryly.

'Having second thoughts?' As the flecked gold eyes pierced her own for a moment, she forced herself to show no reaction to the taunt, waiting a full minute before she replied.

'Second thoughts don't apply to this situation, do they? You forced me to come with you; I had no choice.'

'Not at all,' he said calmly. 'The choice was very clear—take the consequences of your actions or join me for a pleasurable break from routine. I would agree that it wasn't a very difficult choice in the circumstances, but a choice nevertheless.' The hard tawny eyes gleamed at her. 'Don't you agree?' He was close, much too close for comfort.

She shrugged her answer, turning her gaze from his to stare out into the sparkling silver world surrounding them, the trees and bushes proudly displaying their new coats of glittering virginal white, as she struggled to control her traitorous body. 'Don't sulk, Fabia, it's a most unattractive habit.' Her eyes shot up to meet his again and she saw he was smiling coolly as hot colour flooded into her face.

'I'm not sulking,' she said furiously. 'I've got nothing to say and so I'm keeping quiet.'

'A woman who knows when to be quiet?' The dark voice was tauntingly soft. 'There is no end to the surprises that you foist upon me, Miss Grant, is there? A veritable Pandora's box of wonders.' The velvet tones were mockingly warm.

'Oh, shut up.' It was weak, but the best she could do, and for the next few minutes they continued in silence.

Then he spoke again, his deep voice faintly disapproving. 'Haven't you got any boots? You're going to be soaked as soon as we leave the car.'

She flushed at his glance at her tiny feet. 'Of course I've got some boots,' she replied tersely. 'If you remember, it wasn't snowing when we left London and I just didn't choose to wear them.'

'A somewhat unwise decision in the present circumstances.' He slanted a quick glance at her stiff profile. 'And do stop looking as though you're being led to your execution.'

'Why?' she countered quickly. 'That's exactly how I feel.'

'Fabia, Fabia, Fabia...' He sighed mockingly. 'What am I going to do with you?'

'That's exactly what's worrying me,' she said with more than a grain of truth in the sarcasm. She was conscious of his eyes narrowing as all amusement left the hard face, and when he next spoke his voice was devoid of all banter.

'Look, Fabia, there are probably a couple of things we need to get clear,' he said slowly, his eyes intent on the road ahead. Her heart lurched sickeningly as she glanced at the grim face and then her chin rose in unspoken defiance. Here it came, the iron hand in a velvet glove. This was the moment he explained, ever so nicely, the sleeping arrangements...

'The last time we met I wasn't quite myself.' There was a trace of derision in the deep voice but not, she felt, directed at her. 'I may have given you the impression——' He stopped abruptly. 'Well, that last little trick was the straw that broke the camel's back and this particular camel is not known for his patience.' She could believe it. The firm hard mouth was a give-away. 'I have no intention of using you as one of Santa's playmates. You understand me?' She nodded slowly. 'And if this next week isn't going to be a nightmare for us both I would suggest we reach some sort of amicable agreement and keep to it. I will respect your space and you'll respect mine but in public we will be... believable.' The big body was quite motionless.

'How believable?' she asked carefully as her heart pounded.

He gave a harsh bark of a laugh, his expression unreadable. 'You're quite refreshing, you know, like a douse of cold water on a summer's day.' She glanced at him warily, unsure if he was laughing at her or not, but the closed enigmatic face gave nothing away. Her nerves jangled as she looked at him, really looked at him, for the first time that day. Why did he have to be so deliciously attractive? 'I mean it.' The gold eyes flicked over her for a spine-tingling moment. 'Most of the women I know are only too pleased to claim an alliance with the Cade name.' His tone was full of self-mockery and she stared at him for a moment. She didn't understand him, not at all.

'Well, extreme wealth carries its own set of problems, as you've said,' she said quietly. 'That's one of the penalties——'

'There is no need to offer sympathy,' he said scathingly, his voice cutting. 'I'm quite aware of all my assets, Fabia, and how to use them.' She flushed scarlet at the icy rebuff, at the same time as a flood of hot anger turned her eyes brilliant. He was a pig! An autocratic, handsome pig, maybe, but still a pig! 'So...a truce?' She glared at him, but the gesture was lost as he concentrated on the snow-covered road ahead. 'Fabia?' he persisted.

'OK,' she muttered grudgingly. 'If that's what you want.'

'Ah, what I want,' he said thoughtfully. 'Now that is a whole different ball-game, but let's not digress. "Sufficient unto the day" and all that...' He was playing with her, she could feel it. She stared straight ahead into the pale wintry world outside as her thoughts raced. She didn't trust him an inch and especially not when he was being cool and imperturbable, like now. He was so used to everything just falling into his lap! The thought of being on his lap suddenly made her quite hot and she forced her mind into safer areas.

'There's a little pub up ahead,' he said some time later, as the powerful car nosed carefully through the swirling snowstorm which had reached blizzard proportions. 'Fancy a bite to eat?'

She was about to refuse and then realised that his large sturdy frame had been crouched over the wheel of the low-slung sports car for almost two hours while he negotiated them round drifts and past snow-obscured obstacles as they ventured ever deeper into the silent countryside. She had tentatively suggested half an hour ago that it might be wiser to turn back, but the low growl that had greeted her words had dissuaded her from repeating them. 'Lovely,' she said instead, her voice over-bright as he narrowly missed a large bird that flew out of nowhere, wings flapping madly.

'Damn pheasants,' he muttered irritably, and in spite of her concern for the hapless pheasant she felt a quick rush of pleasure that he could be caught off guard like any ordinary mortal. Because he *wasn't* like any other man she had come into contact with! The thought speared her mind and she was glad he was concentrating so hard on his driving and couldn't notice her face. It wasn't his wealth or his influence that attracted the women, she acknowledged silently, but the man himself. He had an aura of mystery, of fascination, aloof and cold and withdrawn at the same time as exuding a bewitching charm that beckoned even as it rebuffed. He was so...complete. She nodded mentally to herself. He was the most complete man she had ever met. Did he have any weaknesses? She doubted it.

'That's it, up ahead, where the lights are.' She looked into the distance and could just make out a faint glimmer now and again in the seconds when the windscreen was clear. 'I could murder those weathermen,' he added grimly. 'This little lot was supposed to hold off until tomorrow. If I'd known we were in for this we could have left yesterday.'

'I couldn't,' she said quickly. 'It was difficult enough to leave two days early for Christmas as it was. I——'

'Oh, you would have, Fabia,' he said quietly without looking at her. 'You would have.' There wasn't a shred of doubt in his voice.

She bit back the hot angry words hovering on her tongue with enormous self-control, realising that at this moment in time he needed all his energy and concentration if they were to make the little inn safely, let alone his grandmother's home.

When they drew into the tiny space in the car park that wasn't covered by mountainous powdery drifts she sighed audibly with relief. 'Thank goodness. I didn't think we'd make it this far back there.'

He glanced at her in surprise, his light brown eyes with their thick lashes enquiring. 'You didn't? But there was no problem.' His face was calm and relaxed.

'No problem?' She stared at him. He seemed even closer now that the engine was stilled and she was conscious of the delicious male smell of aftershave on clean taut skin.

'No problem at all,' he repeated softly, turning in his seat and sliding one arm at the back of her shoulders. 'In the unlikely event that the car should break down I'd carry you to safety. I wouldn't let any harm come to you. Do you believe that?' She sensed he was asking her more than the surface question his words held, and for a moment in time she let her eyes be held by the hypnotic power of his tawny gaze before turning abruptly away, lowering her head so that the silky mass of her hair hid her face from his piercing eyes. He was too close, too...knowing.

'No, I don't think I do,' she said shakily, annoyed to hear the tremor in her voice. If she could hear it, so could he.

'I hope one day you will,' he said softly, so softly that she could barely hear him. She didn't look up and after a moment he opened his door and walked round the car to her side, stopping her as she made to climb out. 'Wait.' Before she realised what he was about to do he had bent down and scooped her out of the warm interior as though she were a small child, straightening with her in his arms and kicking the door shut with his foot.

'Alex! Put me down.' Her voice wasn't as indignant as she would have liked it to be. The feel of his arms about her and the hard strong face just an inch from her own was doing crazy things to her insides, and he was holding her so tightly.

'Why?' He smiled down at her lazily as the snow-flakes fell into the tawny brown richness of his hair. 'You don't want wet feet, do you?' He brushed his lips against the silk of her hair.

Wet feet were the least of her worries at this moment in time, Fabia reflected faintly as he began to walk with her towards the small arched pub door. It felt decep-tively good to be held close to his heart like this, de-ceptive because the rich promise of his big body and strong arms wouldn't be worth the price she would have to pay ultimately. When it ended. As it inevitably would.

He's not Robin, a little voice whispered tantalisingly in her head as they reached the snow-covered steps leading to the pub door, but the other voice was stronger, the voice that said coldly and quite dispassionately that she was here providing a service, for a time. He hadn't even tried to lie about that. She was an available com-modity hired for a specific purpose and when her work was done he would dispatch her back into her own life without another thought. Just like Robin. They came from a different world, these wealthy, spoilt men, a world where they spoke and it was done. She had to remember that, *had to*!

'There we are.' He set her down just outside the door and leant over her to push it open, his snow-covered coat brushing against her face. 'In you go.'

The warmth and colour of a blazing log fire at one end of the small room reached out to greet them as they entered and almost immediately a large burly red-faced giant of a man appeared from a small passageway to one side of the bar. 'Didn't expect anyone to venture out tonight,' he began jovially, his face breaking into a grin as he saw who his customers were. 'Why, it's Mr Cade, isn't it? Come down for the Christmas break, sir? You picked the right day for it!'

'Didn't I just, George,' Alex returned easily with a warm smile. 'Meet Miss Grant. Come to keep me company in case I get lonely.' He turned to Fabia with a wicked gleam in his eyes. 'Isn't that right, sweetheart?'

She looked at him hard for a moment, disliking the innuendo, and then smiled carefully. 'Anything you say, o lord and master. I'm yours to command.' She curtsied prettily, her eyes cold.

George laughed cheerfully in the background, his rough face frankly envious. 'Been trying to get the missus to say that for years,' he said as he began polishing a tray of glasses standing to one side of the ancient till. 'You'll have to let me know your secret some time, Mr Cade.'

Alex smiled at the man as he took Fabia's arm, drawing her over towards the seat by the fire, but she could sense he hadn't liked her little act. It was there in the tightening of his hard jaw and the grip of his fingers on her flesh. 'What would you like to drink? A glass of water?' His smile had a twist in it that she didn't miss, and she glanced up at him defiantly as she sat down, her eyes fiery and her back stiff.

'Anything; I don't mind. They don't do hot drinks, do they?' She shivered as the heat from the fire warmed her cold face. 'I'd love a cup of coffee or hot chocolate.'

'Your wish is my command, o favoured one,' he said softly. 'Who can refuse the favourite of the harem anything?'

She looked up at him warily, her eyes rebellious. 'You started that, Alex,' she said hotly, her face tight. 'Insinuating to that man that I was here as your... your...'

'My what?' His face was genuinely puzzled. 'You're *supposed* to be down here as my girlfriend, for crying out loud, aren't you?'

'You didn't make it sound like that,' she said quickly. 'Not your girlfriend, more... something else.'

'Like hell I did,' he said flatly, his eyes narrowing. 'If any of your other boyfriends had made a remark like that you would have taken it in the spirit it was meant. It was a joke, just a casual everyday joke. You really have got quite a chip on your shoulder where I'm concerned, haven't you? What is it about me, Fabia—my wealth, the lifestyle, my physical appearance? What is it that reminds you so much of him?'

'I've never said there was a "him",' she said coldly, 'and even if there were it's none of your business. You've asked me to do a job and that's what I'm here for. That doesn't give you the right to pry into my personal life.'

'No, you're dead right,' he said icily as he straightened up away from her, his face stony. 'But when you let your personal life interfere with the work in hand it becomes my business, and that's exactly what you're doing. I don't care whether you like me or not but we might as well get it clear now that I won't tolerate snide remarks and sarcasm for a week. I meant nothing by what I said and whether you believe me or not you're going to have to accept that. I've no intention of watching everything I say for the next few days in case you take offence. Got it?' He marched over to the bar before she could reply and she sat where she was, cheeks burning and hands clenched in impotent rage.

As her cheeks cooled along with her anger she was forced to admit to herself, albeit reluctantly, that he did have a point. She wouldn't have taken umbrage at the remark from anyone else, it was true. She eyed him with distinct irritation as he stood talking to George at the bar. She was in the wrong, again! Why do you have to be so altogether perfect? she thought balefully as she stared at him across the room. And why can you read me like a book? She suddenly wished with all her heart that she hadn't agreed to this crazy idea. She should have let him do his worst, let him unleash his anger—anything rather than be with him like this. She was standing on the edge of a precipice and it felt as if she were blindfolded.

'One cup of coffee.' As he placed the steaming cup in front of her she blinked and realised with a start that she hadn't seen him cross the room. 'Dreaming?' He smiled slowly, the cold anger of a few minutes before seemingly evaporated.

'I'm sorry, Alex.' She spoke quickly before she lost her nerve. 'I was being touchy. I can see you didn't mean anything in what you said.' She touched his arm in a gesture of apology.

He sat down beside her, a strange expression on his face as his eyes rested on the small hand resting on his arm. He smiled slowly. 'And you apologise when you're wrong? You really are quite an enigma, Miss Fabia Grant. I'm not at all sure if it was a good day or a bad day for me when you blazed over my horizon.'

'Blazed?' She risked a shaky smile. There had been something in the deep voice, something tender, that she preferred not to dwell on. It stirred too many discarded dreams.

'Definitely blazed,' he said lazily. 'You stood out from the other women like——'

'Shall we eat?' She broke in with a smile to soften the abruptness but she couldn't listen to any more. Those had been the very words Robin had said to her all those years ago. 'You stood out from the other women like an exotic flower in a field of daisies'. She hadn't understood at the time that some men were fascinated by a challenge, the unattainable, but later, much later, how she had envied those daisies.

'Sure.' She sensed those sharp gold eyes missed nothing, but he accepted the change of conversation gracefully as he settled back in his seat. 'The steak in red wine sauce is excellent here. George's brother is a butcher and George gets preferential treatment for all the best cuts of meat. Care to try it?'

'Thank you.' She passed him the menu, her face enquiring. 'Do you often eat here, then?'

'I normally stop off and see old George if I'm down this way,' he said blandly, his eyes narrowing on her surprised face. 'I grew up in this neck of the woods, remember.'

'Yes.' She looked at him carefully. 'Of course.'

'You find that surprising?' There was a soft note in his voice that warned her she was on dangerous ground and she hesitated for a moment before answering him.

'Not exactly.' She chose her words cautiously. 'It's just so different from your normal sort of place... that restaurant in London, you know...' As her voice trailed away he didn't move for a long moment, looking at her silently from frosted eyes.

'No, I don't know, Fabia. Do I take it you assume I'm the sort of clown who only likes to be seen in the "right" places? Who carries a social *Who's Who* in his pocket? Is that it?'

It was so close to what she did think, how Robin had behaved, that a flood of betraying colour stained her cheeks pink.

'I see.' His voice was still cool and quiet but his eyes were deadly. 'Charming. And how did you arrive at this delightful piece of supposition? No, let me guess.' He held up his hand mockingly. 'It's none of my business, right?'

She stared at him miserably. The last couple of hours had been a wonderful start to the holiday!

'Well, let's just suppose, for a short while, that there are a few things about me you don't know? Ridiculous, you're thinking, but humour me.' The contempt in his voice was matched only by the scorn in his face. 'I am— surprise, surprise—quite normal in some respects. I eat, I sleep, I breathe and if you cut me I bleed.' He smiled coldly. 'I enjoy doing ordinary things,' he continued, his voice lifted in exaggerated surprise. 'I sometimes drive my own car, take the dogs for a walk, go to the pub. I even——' he paused dramatically '—cook a meal for myself now and again. "What?" you're asking. "This leader of the social whirl, this heartless seducer of women—can this be true?"' He paused and took a deep breath. 'I work hard and I play hard and I don't intend to apologise to you for either.' She stared at him silently, quite unable to speak. 'And for crying out loud stop looking at me like that!'

He moved so violently that his chair scraped harshly against the red tiles of the hearth, and as George raised his grizzled head in surprise Alex forced a smile to his face. 'Two steaks in red wine, George, and a nice bottle of wine, OK?'

'OK, Mr Cade. Ten minutes.'

Fabia sat in stunned silence for a few seconds more and then opened her mouth to speak at the same moment as she caught his eye. 'Not a word, Fabia, not a word.'

She flushed angrily. 'I was only——'

'I said not a word.' She suddenly understood how he controlled his empire. There was a savage ruthlessness in his voice that stopped her in her tracks. She didn't dare speak! She was furious and she wanted to, but she didn't dare. She glared at him nevertheless, her dark blue eyes flashing sparks. 'And drink your coffee.' There was a thread of amusement in the dark voice that seared her stretched nerves like fire. 'You can rest assured that your objections, although not verbal, have been taken note of.'

They didn't speak again until George brought their meal. Alex seemed perfectly calm and untroubled, his big body relaxed and easy and his dark, handsome face quiet. She, on the other hand, Fabia reflected bitterly, was as tight as a coiled spring! It wasn't fair. None of this was fair!

The meal was delicious but she could only eat a small portion of the succulent meat and one potato. There was a huge lump in her throat that defied all food and the churning in her stomach was rendering eating impossible.

'What's the matter?' She became aware that his eyes were fixed on her face as she moved a piece of steak around on her plate for the umpteenth time. 'Are you worried about meeting my grandmother?'

Your grandmother? For an awful moment she thought she had voiced her amazement out loud. His grandmother was the last person she was concerned about, she thought wryly as she looked into the tawny gold eyes. If she were Lucretia Borgia personified the lady would be a pussycat to handle beside this man.

'I'm just not hungry,' she answered quietly. 'Too much breakfast.'

His eyes were frankly disbelieving. 'You'll be all right.' He reached out a hand suddenly and touched her arm gently. 'I told you, I won't let any harm come to you.'

His eyes held hers in a tight grip. 'Trust me.' Her flesh tingled faintly where he'd touched.

'I can't.' It was a faint whisper and for a long moment they were locked in a silent world of their own.

'I could kill him.' His voice was flat. 'Whoever he was or is I could kill him. He's here with us now, isn't he?'

'Please don't,' she said weakly. It wasn't real, this concern, this caring. She lowered her eyes, stroking the top of her wine glass distractedly. She had been here before. She mustn't forget. Physical attraction meant little to a man like him.

When they left the cosy shelter of the small, warm pub it was to find that although the worst of the blizzard had abated an icy northerly wind was slicing the air with savage fingers and it was quite dark. Alex lifted her into his arms without a word and this time she didn't protest, steeling herself to show no emotion when he set her down by the car, his face tight.

'One thing, Fabia.' There was a strange tenseness in his voice and his arms were still about her as he spoke, his breath a white cloud on the frosty air. 'Which is it?'

'What?' She stared up at him in the circle of his arms, her eyes dark midnight-blue and her hair a pale glow in the darkness. 'I don't understand...'

'No, of course.' His voice was husky. 'I'm not expressing myself very well. This man, is he a "was" or an "is"?' His eyes were piercingly intent on her face. 'It's not idle curiosity, I need to know. The present circumstances and so on...' It was almost as though he wanted to say more and she waited a moment, her heart pounding and her hands clammy in spite of the freezing air. She wished he would kiss her... The thought jolted her out of the odd stillness that seemed to have her in its grasp and she shut her eyes for a brief moment before replying.

'Was.' She looked up and caught a flash of emotion in his eyes seconds before a shutter came down and blanked it out. 'He's a was.'

'Right.' Although he hadn't moved a muscle and his facial expression was just the same she felt he had changed, that some pressure, a tautness, had drained away. He opened the car door without letting go of her, easing her into the seat, and reaching into the back for a big fluffy car-rug which he draped about her lap before shutting the door carefully. He didn't speak when he joined her a moment later, starting the engine and clearing the windows of their burden of icy snow in silence.

As they continued on their way along white deserted roads the wind was vicious in its intensity, stirring the powdery flakes of snow that had settled on trees and bushes into mad flurries now and again and jostling the car with its force. They passed the odd solitary car crawling along at a pace to match theirs but otherwise the world seemed quite empty, the starlit clear sky overhead and the cold white earth beneath in perfect harmony.

'We've made it.' She came to with a start and realised she must have been dozing; the cosy warmth of the car had been deliciously seductive. She looked about her with wide eyes, seeing nothing but a huge snow-covered stone wall in which were set an enormous pair of wrought-iron gates.

'We have?' She realised there had been a note of great thankfulness in his voice although he had displayed no anxiety or concern during the journey at all. But then he wouldn't, would he? she thought intuitively. She was beginning to realise that Alexander Cade was not an easy man to understand. 'I don't see anything.'

'No, the house is down the drive a way, but first . . .' He cut the engine and leant over towards her, taking her lips in a firm, hard kiss before she could move. As his mouth covered hers she knew she wouldn't resist, that she didn't want to resist, that she had been waiting for this moment all day. 'So sweet, so fresh...' His passion was growing as he felt her response to him, his tongue plundering her mouth and his hands crushing her against him so that her hair hung in a golden veil over his arm.

The kiss was all-consuming and like before it amazed her with its power, a sweet drugging sensation taking hold of her senses as she melted into him, her hands caught against his hard chest and her head bent backwards. He was running his hands up and down her back now as he covered her eyes, cheeks and mouth in tiny burning kisses, his breathing harsh and uneven.

'Fabia?' There was a note of undisguised surprise in his voice as she opened her eyes to find his face an inch away from hers. She sensed that the blazing passion that had sprung up between them the moment he had touched her lips with his had taken him by surprise as much as it had amazed her. Surely people didn't normally feel like this? This wasn't usual, was it? She stared at him, her eyes huge in her pink-tinted face.

'I was going to kiss you and say I hope you'll have a wonderful Christmas,' he said ruefully as he let go of her, moving back into his seat slowly and brushing a lock of tawny-brown hair off his forehead. 'The...ardour wasn't premeditated.'

'Thank you,' she said shakily, quite unable to muster a casual reply to ease the situation. 'I hope you have a good Christmas too.'

'Yes.' He stared at her for another long moment before turning the ignition key so that the car sprang into life, easing his way between the gates and on to a long tree-lined drive that seemed to stretch into the distance forever, winding and turning as it went. Someone had obviously cleared the drive of snow in anticipation of their arrival; it was heaped in great shining banks either side of them and there was a thin scattering of dark sand beneath the car's tyres. It was a full minute before the house came into view and when it did it merely added to the sense of unreality that had taken hold of her in the last few hours.

The building was palatial, huge and regally beautiful in mellow white stone, set on a slight incline with massive weathered oaks either side like dutiful sentries. It was grand, imposing, like a magnificent stately home, and as she looked at it she felt slightly sick. I must be mad! she thought faintly. This cool, controlled man at her side had grown up in surroundings fit for a king, as far removed from her beginnings as it was possible to imagine, and here she was thinking that he might just be different from Robin, that perhaps he could be genuine.

You fool, she thought harshly. You stupid, pathetic fool. You have maybe caught his fancy for a brief moment in time, something different in his normal well ordered life that he can turn to his advantage, but don't forget you're here doing a job, no more, no less. You couldn't begin to function in his world; you don't even know the ground rules. She remembered the last words Robin had flung at her as she had left the flat that day, with the sound of his mistress's sobs in the background. 'You didn't seriously think you were expected to last, did you? You were a change, my dear, like good old-fashioned ice-cream after an excess of soufflé.' His face had been cruel, red with frustrated passion and rage, the short bathrobe he had pulled on to cover his nakedness revealing white hairless legs that were curiously repugnant. She had concentrated on his legs for a long time, she reflected bitterly; it had helped to get the rest of the miserable fiasco into balance.

'Penny for them?' As they glided to a halt in front of the massive oak door flanked by two imposing stone lions at the top of the circular steps Fabia raised her eyes to Alex's watching face, her expression guarded.

'They aren't worth a penny.' She smiled carefully. 'I would be robbing you.'

'I doubt that.' He was looking at her hard, his eyes noting the tight line of her lips and shadowed eyes, her hands bunched nervously in her lap. 'I doubt that very much. You intrigue me, Miss Fabia Grant; I've never met a woman who houses so many different facets in one lovely body. Playful, wicked, defensive, vulnerable...which is the real you?' She stared at him without answering, her eyes almost black against the whiteness of her face. 'But maybe they are all you?' he continued thoughtfully. 'A grand composite of a hundred men's dreams just waiting to be released.'

'There's nothing mystical about me, I assure you, so don't waste your time trying to make me into something I'm not,' she said sharply, the colour returning to her face as her anger sent a burst of welcome adrenalin to banish the past and provide help for the present. 'I'm a perfectly ordinary average working girl with two flat feet firmly on the ground. You needn't try to charm me into thinking I'm something wonderful, Mr Cade. I know what I am.'

'Maybe.' He smiled slowly. 'But do you know *who* you are? That's different, my prickly little siren. I have a feeling that the real Fabia Grant is in there somewhere, just waiting to be let out. She just got lost for a while.'

'Look——'

He cut her indignant response off with a lazy chuckle. 'And the name is Alex, angel-face, remember? I hardly think ''Mr Cade'' holds sufficient warmth to make our relationship believable, do you?'

She looked at him as he sat, perfectly relaxed and self-assured, long dark hair perfectly groomed and gleaming against the black coat and his tawny eyes glittering at her discomfiture, and felt a moment's blinding panic at what she had taken on. But it was too late now. As the big door at the top of the steps swung open the thought repeated itself like a ominous tolling bell. It was far, far too late.

CHAPTER FIVE

THE next few minutes were a confused jumble of larger than life images and noise which gradually sorted themselves into order as they stood in the baronial splendour of the vast hall. The seeming crowd of people that had surrounded them as they had stepped out of Alex's car had shrunk into four elderly servants plus two huge German shepherd dogs which were clearly delighted to see Alex and ignored her with magnificent disregard.

'This is Mary.' Alex hugged the small plump grey-haired woman whose plain face was wreathed in a beaming smile of welcome. 'Best housekeeper in the world, eh, Mary?' The little woman giggled and pushed at him with the flat of her hand.

'Oh, you, Mr Alex, always the flatterer!'

'And this is Jenny, who cooks for us, and Christine, my grandmother's companion.' The two elderly women bobbed their heads smilingly. 'And to keep this house of females in order I rely on the very capable services of John.' He shook the ageing butler's hand as he spoke. 'How is she, John?'

'Looking forward to seeing you, sir.' John was obviously of the old school, Fabia reflected silently as the tall elderly man bowed his head to her solemnly, his face carefully polite. Somehow he seemed the odd one out in this atmosphere of easy informality where even the dogs seemed part of one huge family.

She had a moment's vivid recollection of Robin's coldness with what he termed 'inferiors', which had frequently bordered on rudeness. It had been one of the many things which she had pushed to the back of her mind at the time, dazzled and bewitched as she had been, but which had made perfect sense after the event.

'We'd better go straight in or else she'll be complaining we've kept her waiting,' Alex said smilingly to John, who nodded approvingly, a slight smile touching the severe line of his thin mouth.

'Very wise, sir.'

'Hey, behave, you two.' He stopped after two steps, his hand holding Fabia's arm, and turned to the two dogs, who had slunk behind them ingratiatingly. 'You know you aren't allowed in the drawing-room. Take them into my sitting-room, John—I'll be along in a few minutes.'

'Very good, sir.' When John, the dogs and the three women had disappeared, making the huge hall even larger, he turned to her, his eyes warm, his arms slipping casually round her waist.

'That wasn't too bad, was it?' he asked softly, his gaze drifting to her mouth and then back to her wide-eyed stare as she struggled to take in the opulence of her surroundings.

'No, they seem very nice,' she said weakly.

'Salt of the earth,' he agreed immediately. 'They've all been with my grandmother for years, John since she came to the house as a young and very nervous bride some sixty-five years ago, although he was just a kitchen boy then. He's absolutely devoted to her although she plagues him unmercifully.'

'Is that all the household?' she asked as he walked with her along the hall, pausing in front of a pair of beautifully carved oak doors with curving, ornate brass handles.

'No.' He looked down at her slowly. 'With a house this size it takes some upkeep, so there are a couple of women who come in from the village a few times a week to clean and then two gardeners who double as chauffeurs when necessary. They don't live in.'

'Oh.' Her voice was flat.

'You knew my financial situation, Fabia,' he said softly, lifting her chin so her gaze was forced to meet his. 'What did you expect?' His eyes raked her troubled face intently.

'I don't know.' She shook her head distractedly. 'It's just so... I don't know if I can be what you want me to be for your grandmother.' Blue eyes met gold defiantly.

'I want you to be yourself,' he said firmly, his eyes hooded. 'And don't forget this is an estate that has been in the Cade family for generations; we have no choice in the matter. I would prefer to just have my house in London and the couple of properties abroad, but there it is...' His eyes narrowed on her face. 'My ancestors would haunt me if I let it go.'

'You?' She paused uncertainly. 'But I thought it was your grandmother's home?'

'So it is.' He nodded confirmation. 'But with death duties and other annoying liabilities my grandmother made the estate over to me lock, stock and barrel when I was twenty-one. She didn't expect to live so long.' He smiled at her face. 'Should I have refused it then?'

'No, of course not.' She lowered her eyes quickly. 'And I didn't mean to pry, this is none of my business.' She raised her head as a sudden thought struck her. 'She must have trusted you very much, to give you everything like that.'

'We love each other,' he said simply, his eyes fixed piercingly on her confused face as he opened the doors quietly. 'There's perfect trust where the heart is involved.'

'And about time!' The voice that greeted them was strong and loud, a total antithesis to the tiny, shrivelled-up little figure seated in the massive armchair at the far end of the room almost on top of a huge blazing fire. 'Where have you been? Gossiping with John about me, no doubt? Don't you believe a thing that fool of a doctor has told him, Alexander! I've no intention of dying yet.'

'I've brought someone to meet you, Grandmama,' Alex said stolidly, patently ignoring the whole content of the tiny woman's words as he urged Fabia forward, his arm holding her close to his side.

'I can see that.' Isabella Cade glared at her grandson from the depths of the armchair. 'I might be old and disagreeable, Alexander, but I am *not* senile! Come here, my dear.'

The change in both voice and appearance as the old woman smiled beguilingly at her caught Fabia by surprise and she blinked nervously, glad of the support of Alex's arm as they walked down the beautifully furnished, opulent room, her feet sinking into the thick cream carpet which was ankle-deep.

'This is Miss Fabia Grant, Grandmama; she has agreed to spend Christmas with us.' Alex's voice was almost without expression as they stopped in front of the small figure, his face calm and smiling, but Fabia had eyes for no one but the diminutive little woman staring back at her so interestedly, bright black button eyes and thick white hair belying her great age. She looked like an old, and very mischievous, little gnome.

'Miss Fabia Grant.' The strong, slightly aristocratic voice repeated her name slowly. 'And do you work for your living, Miss Grant?' The lined, paper-thin face stared up at her.

Fabia blinked again in surprise, the formal introductory small talk she had rehearsed in her mind dying in the path of such directness. 'Yes, I do, Mrs Cade,' she said clearly and firmly. 'I am an advertising executive in a large firm.'

'Is that a real job or just one Daddy has purchased for you?' The piercing black eyes were holding her soft violet ones tight now, and as Fabia felt Alex tense by her side and open his mouth to speak she intervened quickly, her voice staunch and unflinching. Grandmother or not, she would deal with this herself!

'It's a real job, Mrs Cade, worked for *by* myself *for* myself with no help from anyone else at all.' She held the tiny woman's glance unwaveringly. 'That's the way I like it.'

'Looking the way you do?' The tone was faintly disbelieving. 'I can't believe there haven't been many men who would have liked to smooth your path.' The beady eyes flickered over her face.

'I wouldn't deny it.' Fabia was pale-faced and unsmiling now. 'Unfortunately, even in today's liberated society, there are still some men who are egotistical enough to consider a woman as a body with cotton wool for a brain, and, *more* unfortunately, still some women who agree with that opinion.' She held the hard eyes fast. 'You know the sort of woman I mean, Mrs Cade?' It was a blunt criticism and the ancient face knew it.

Young and old stared into each other's minds for a long searching moment and then Isabella Cade sank back into her cushions tiredly, patting the arm of her chair with a tiny wrinkled frail hand. 'I like you, Fabia. I can call you Fabia, can't I?' Fabia nodded dumbly, dazed by the mercurial change of mood. 'I was worried when you walked in that door that you would be a flopsy with no mind of her own or a poor little rich girl becrying Daddy's millions. But you are neither of those things, are you, Miss Fabia Grant?' The old lady smiled wickedly at her grandson who was shaking his head slightly. 'And stop glaring at me, Alexander. I'm too long in the tooth to change and you should allow an old woman her indulgences.'

'Age has nothing to do with it, Grandmama, as you well know,' Alex said severely with just the trace of a smile to soften his words. 'You've always been the same; your age has just grown into your tongue now and is a convenient excuse.'

'Very convenient.' She smiled roguishly, turning back to Fabia now and looking up at her enquiringly. 'Do you like my grandson, Fabia?' The meaning was painfully clear and now Alex stepped in firmly, his tone abrupt and his face losing the indulgent expression it had hitherto held.

'Enough, Isabella!'

'He only calls me that when I've overstepped the mark,' the bright voice explained to Fabia comfortably, 'although I don't see why in this case. Still, no matter.' The scrawny hands pulled the knitted shawl covering her legs more closely round her. 'Do you find it chilly, Fabia?'

The heat from the fire was enough to roast one alive, Fabia thought faintly. Already she could feel her cheeks glowing scarlet and small beads of moisture dampening her upper lip. 'It's icy outside,' she said quickly, parrying the question adroitly with a nod to the curtained windows.

'Tactful too.' The wafer-thin hand lifted slowly to pat her tentatively on her arm. 'I didn't feel the cold at your age either, but this miserable collection of bones lets me down now.' The deep-socketed eyes closed slowly. 'I'm feeling a little tired, children. Run away and play until dinner.'

As Alex signalled to Fabia to rise he bent and kissed the top of the white head gently, his eyes tender. 'Till dinner, then, you wicked old lady.'

'You wouldn't have me any different,' his grandmother returned immediately, still with her eyes shut.

'Is she always like that?' Fabia asked weakly as they entered Alex's private sitting-room at the back of the house a few minutes later.

'Always.' He gestured for her to be seated in one of the big winged armchairs pulled close to the crackling log fire in front of which both dogs had been stretched comfortably until their arrival when they had leapt up to greet Alex, long furry tails wagging and tongues lolling ridiculously.

'These are Major and Minor, by the way, father and son.' He stroked the long fur for a few seconds before snapping his fingers, at which signal both dogs slunk back to their original position. 'They're supposed to be guard dogs, bought to swell the effectiveness of the security system, but are both as soft as butter. Everyone blames me.' He smiled at her, his white teeth flashing in his tanned face and the gold eyes creasing at the corners. She caught her breath suddenly as she stared into his face. Why couldn't he have been ordinary, an everyday man working hard for his daily bread and butter? Why did he have to be so far out of her reach? Her eyes widened at the path her thoughts were following and she slammed a door shut in her mind with ferocious determination.

'Just hearing them bark would be enough for the average burglar,' she said lightly, reaching down to pat one noble head. 'And seeing them would do the trick; they're quite magnificent.'

'Long-haired German shepherds are beautiful dogs,' he agreed softly without taking his eyes off her flushed face. She had the feeling that although they were talking quite normally something had sprung up between them that was curiously intimate in its intensity. 'She liked you, you know—you made quite a hit.' She stared at him as he took a step nearer. 'But I knew she would. The first time I saw you——'

She laughed nervously, trying to dispel the mood. 'The first moment you saw me? I seem to remember you avoided me after that first moment all evening.'

'I should have trusted my initial instincts,' he said slowly as he reached her side and drew her up by her hand until she was standing within the circle of his arms. 'They've never let me down yet.' The moment to resist was there but she let it slip away.

This time his embrace was hard and fierce, and as his head lowered to take her lips she knew a moment's breathtaking panic before the feel of his mouth drove all lucid thought from her mind. He's done this so many times before, he's too good at it! The thought hammered in her mind but in spite of his expertise she couldn't help responding feverishly as he pulled her into his body, moulding her to the hard firm planes of his male frame, leaving her in no doubt as to the desire she had raised in him. His mouth was ravaging hers in an agony of need now and that tiny part of her she had kept locked away since Robin's cruelty had broken the key suddenly unlocked in a sweet response that had her straining against him, giving back kiss for kiss, moaning softly as his lips searched every contour of her hot face, wanting more as his hands travelled over her body in gentle exploration, his flesh warm against hers.

'You are so beautiful, my darling...' As he murmured quiet words of endearment against her lips she found herself wanting to believe him, wanting to trust him. She was so tired of being alone, of fighting her natural yearning for someone to share things with, someone to belong to... Her breath was coming in sobbing pants now and she wound her arms tightly round his neck, revelling in the smell, the feel, the completeness of him. It would be all right. She needed it to be all right. He wasn't Robin, he wasn't at all like Robin. And she wanted to trust him.

'Mr Alexander?' The polite knock at the door took them both by surprise and as Alex moved her from him she knew a moment's deep, blindingly strong protest inside her. 'I have your tea-trolley, sir.'

'Just a moment, John.' As Alex raked back his hair with hard fingers and smoothed his tie into place she wondered at his composure. He was so cool, so unruffled, whereas she felt as if... Her cheeks burnt still hotter. She felt as if he had already made love to her. She sat down abruptly in the chair she had vacated, adjusting her clothing with shaking hands before bending quickly to stroke Major's coarse, springy fur as Alex opened the door. She didn't know herself any more. How could he sweep away seven years of hard-won cool remoteness in half as many weeks? This was madness, but oh, so sweet.

As John served them tea her cheeks cooled and the trembling deep inside that his passion had induced quietened. As the old man left, the little housekeeper came bustling in with a pot of water to replenish the teapot, loading their plates with still further sandwiches and cake, and standing to chat while they ate. She sensed that Alex wanted to tell the small woman to leave but his innate courtesy won through and he talked amiably with Mary, who was clearly delighted to have 'Mr Alex' home, her round cheeks bobbing animatedly and her brown eyes soft with pleasure.

'I'll show you your room. I'm sure you would like to have a rest before dinner.' As Mary wheeled the tea-trolley from the room he took her arm, leading her to another huge winding staircase at the back of the house.

'I'll get lost here.' The moment of closeness had passed and she needed time now to formulate this new thing that was happening, take in the enormity of what she was feeling. 'I've never been in such a huge place.' She shrugged his arm away carefully.

'It is vast,' he agreed lightly with a discerning glance at her pale face, 'but your rooms are close to the main staircase so you can't go far wrong. I'll show you around properly later.' He didn't press her to acknowledge their earlier intimacy and for that she was grateful as he led her along several thickly carpeted corridors hung with beautifully framed pictures and dotted with small upholstered easy-chairs in tiny alcoves. 'We've come the long way,' he said as he drew to a halt outside a door identical to the others they had passed. 'The main stairs are just down there but if you get lost, shout.'

'I doubt if anyone would hear me,' she said quietly as he opened the door to reveal what looked like a suite of rooms, the small sitting-room they stepped into regal in white and gold.

'Oh, I'd hear you, Fabia,' he said softly, his voice husky and low. 'You could go to the ends of the earth and I'd still hear you if you called for me.' He moved to take her in his arms but she backed away suddenly, the tenderness and desire in his eyes causing an alarm she couldn't hide.

'I'm rushing you.' He stopped immediately and turned from her, his voice controlled now with its customary coolness. 'I didn't mean to; I planned...' He stopped and straightened his shoulders before turning to her, his face distant now and very cold. 'I'll see you later at dinner, eight o'clock.'

When the door shut behind him and she was really alone she suddenly felt as though her legs couldn't hold her any more. She sank on to a small, heavily embroidered chair in soft gold as she glanced round the room distractedly. It was beautiful, like everything else here. She shut her eyes for an instant and breathed deeply. 'This is crazy, you know it's crazy,' she said out loud, the sound of her voice bringing her eyes open with a quick snap. 'Look around you, girl, just open your eyes and look. What could he possibly want with you, apart from a quick fling for convenience's sake?' She shut her eyes again as the thoughts hammered relentlessly in her mind. But he was different, she felt he was different... She sat for a long time in the quietness of the graceful room, the soft warming glow from the wall-lights reflecting back the gold of the heavy brocade curtains, which had been pulled to banish the cold world outside. She had never felt so confused in her life.

After a time she wandered into the large and very ornate bathroom, deciding to have a bath and luxuriate in the sumptuous surroundings rather than a quick shower. Half an hour later, with her wet hair swathed in a small hand-towel and her body enfolded in a warm fluffy bath-sheet, she padded through again to the sitting-room and through to the bedroom beyond, opening the large walk-in wardrobe and wondering what to wear as she gazed at her entire stock of clothes which seemed lost in the vastness.

The sound of high laughter beneath the window caught her attention and made her stiffen. Hugging the towel tightly round her, she walked across to the curtains and pulled them aside, peering down the ivy-covered stone wall outside to the snow-covered drive. She could just see a woman standing in the light from the house, the drifting snowflakes that were caught in the slight breeze now the storm had burnt itself out falling on to sleek black hair and the lovely young upturned face. She laughed again, her full red lips a soft pout in the whiteness of her face, and although Fabia couldn't see her expression clearly in the dim light she felt the beautiful face was alight with some emotion, alive with feeling. It was the girl from the reception, his girlfriend!

As Alex stepped into view, taking the woman's arm in the way he had so often taken hers, she felt no shred of surprise. With a feeling of doom she realised she had expected the inevitable from the first moment the carefree laughter had met her ears. It had been too good to be true, the hope, the expectation. She had known really, deep inside.

She wanted to turn away but remained glued to the window in an agony of self-torture. He walked the woman over to a Land Rover parked haphazardly to one side of the drive, bending down to hear something she was saying so the lighter brown of his hair merged with the darkness of hers. As she saw the woman's arms come round his neck and Alex's head being drawn down to meet the half-open bright red lips Fabia shot away from the window as though it had burnt her, the towel falling from her hair and the damp golden strands tumbling down on to the bare skin of her shoulders.

'Fool, fool, fool...' She ground the words out through tightly clenched teeth as she strode round the room in an agony of feeling before collapsing on the softness of the bed. 'It doesn't matter, he means nothing to you.' She was talking to herself in earnest now but she didn't care, she reflected wildly as she buried her face in the sweet-smelling duvet. There was nothing to get upset about; he hadn't done anything after all, had he? Hadn't promised a thing. She sat up suddenly, her eyes widening in shock. Just the opposite, in fact! He had been absolutely honest with her when he had explained his reasons for wanting her to accompany him here. He needed someone who was quite clear as to where she stood, no strings attached and certainly *not* heart-strings. She pulled his words out of the depths of her mind. 'I am in the middle of several important business transactions and can't waste time on trivia.' She bit her lip hard. What had he said? Oh, yes, he didn't want 'interminable problems once the festive season is over'. That woman down there, there were probably lots more like her and now he was counting her as of the same ilk. She tasted blood in her mouth. How could she have been so stupid? Of course he wouldn't say no to a little light diversion during her stay here; what man would? Of course he was going to try it on and see how she responded. And had she responded! She groaned as she kicked at the duvet viciously with her legs. But she hadn't meant it like that, she had felt——

She froze on the bed. What had she felt? She sat up, her hair a tangled mass of gold around her heart-shaped face in which her eyes shone out a vivid violet-blue in the whiteness. 'I felt a darn sight too much,' she murmured in the emptiness. But it was just physical attraction, of course it was. She nodded vigorously. The raw sexuality between them couldn't be denied but from this moment on she would keep it in its place. If she couldn't be remembered for anything else he would remember her as the one he *didn't* sleep with!

By the time she was ready for dinner she was the epitome of the cool blonde, long golden hair swept into a soft loose bun on the top of her head and a little discreet make-up to give some colour to her over-pale face. She had bought two new evening dresses, along with a long black skirt and several glittery tops, expecting they would dress for dinner each night, and now the soft gold silk of the ridiculously expensive dress gave her the courage she needed to face him again. She looked good, she knew she did, and for the moment that was all she must think of. She had brought this whole mess on herself, she would admit that, but she was blowed if she was going to become one of Alexander Cade's 'fancies'. 'No way, Mr Cade,' she said bitterly into the mirror as she checked herself for the last time. 'You're just like all the rest; the only difference with you is that you're honest about it. Well, thanks for the warning. I shan't forget again.' The tenderness, the sweet words, they were a familiar pattern, probably genuine at the time but swiftly forgotten. How easy it had been to persuade herself differently.

She eased her mouth into a smile as she caught its tightness in the mirror. He had told her he was a busy man with no time for commitment. Well, fine; that suited her just fine! He had nothing she wanted. She despised all his kind.

Her thoughts were mirrored on her face as she opened the door, starting visibly as she almost cannoned into the focus of her malevolence, who was standing just outside, hand raised to knock. 'What's happened?' The smile on his face died as his rapier-sharp glance swept over her face seconds before she schooled her features into blankness.

'Happened?' She forced a short laugh and then wished she hadn't as the sound died in a croak. 'Nothing's happened.'

'You're upset.' He looked at her keenly. 'You weren't like this when I left you a couple of hours ago.'

Before I saw you in a passionate clinch with Miss Happy-Go-Lucky? she thought balefully. How dared he? How dared he look at her as though he really cared how she felt when just half an hour before he had held another woman in his arms? She still wasn't quite sure what his little game was but she didn't like it, she didn't like it at all!

'Nonsense.' She smiled casually. 'You just startled me, that's all.'

'Well, if you look like that when you're startled, angel-face, I sure dread to think how you appear when you're angry.' He leant back against the far wall as he spoke, his eyes lazy as they wandered over her slender form. 'You look gorgeous, absolutely gorgeous, by the way.'

Cut the charm, she thought to herself angrily, this girl's immune. 'I'm here to do a job and I intend to do it to the best of my ability,' she said coolly, driving back all treacherous thoughts of how delicious he looked in his evening suit with rigid determination. 'You kept your part of the arrangement; now I do my bit, OK?'

He straightened abruptly, the warmth in his face dying as he took in her stony face and hard voice. 'I see, a business deal, nothing else. That's what this little episode is trying to tell me, right?' She nodded coldly. 'And the little scene in the sitting-room? That meant nothing, I suppose?'

'Absolutely nothing.'

'What is it with you, Fabia?' He took a step towards her and then seemed to force himself to stand still, his big body taut and restrained. 'Why are we back to the ice-maiden act? It won't wash any more. I know you want me as much as I want you. I felt your need downstairs when we were making love.'

'We weren't doing anything of the sort,' she said icily as inside her whole being jolted with the force of his words. So he thought he only had to click his fingers and she would succumb, did he? The arrogance! The sheer male arrogance! 'We exchanged a few kisses, that's all; "love" had nothing to do with it! That phrase is dreadfully misused.'

'Well, excuse me...' he drawled slowly, resuming his former position against the wall, his eyes hooded against her. Somehow she felt the casual stance was a pose, a sham, but then she couldn't trust her feelings where he was concerned. The last few hours had made that plain. 'Do I take it you are still prepared to play the part allotted to you in public?' She nodded again, her eyes wary. 'Well, that's good of you, that's really benevolent,' he said smoothly. 'But let me make one thing plain, Fabia— I thought I already had but it would appear you had missed my point.' The gold eyes had turned to marble. 'In private there is no need to continue the charade. I'm not starved of female companionship, as you well know.'

His face was expressionless but she suddenly knew, without a shadow of a doubt, that he was furiously angry. 'Neither would I intentionally force myself where I'm not wanted. I obviously misunderstood your...enthusiasm for the role as something else. Nevertheless you are here and you'll behave yourself in front of my grandmother. Do you understand me?'

'Perfectly.' She glared at him furiously and for a long moment they were like two contestants in a boxing-ring seconds before the bell went for the next round.

'Hell, Fabia,' he shook his head as he levered himself off the wall, 'why do I always bite back with you? Look, I don't know what's going on in that head of yours but how about giving me a break, girl? Letting down the drawbridge for just a short time? You don't know me, fine, I accept that, but how about throwing out all the preconceived rubbish that you've taken in and giving us a chance to get to know each other better? If nothing else it's going to make the next few days a lot easier for everyone concerned.'

For a moment, just a moment, the sincerity in his deep rich voice reached her and she felt herself weakening, and then the icy hand of logic pulled her backwards with a sharp jerk. Fool, she told herself bitterly, how many times do you have to be burnt before you stop playing with fire? The man's lethal. You thought Robin had got a good line but he was a mere novice beside Alex.

'I'm here to do a job for you and nothing else,' she repeated as she shut the door behind her, turning back to see his face close against her, his features setting into the cold autocratic lines she knew so well.

'OK, Fabia, have it your way,' he said unemotionally, his eyes looking through her as they walked along the corridor. 'If you want to live in that little box you've made for yourself, who am I to try and dissuade you?' The tone was casual and uncaring and hurt her more

than anything that had gone before, but she said nothing.
Her emotions were too raw for more verbal sparring.

Isabella was sitting in solitary splendour as they entered the huge dining-room, a tiny little figure at the end
of the vast dining-table, and somehow, in spite of the
little woman's caustic tongue, the sight touched Fabia
deeply.

'You look quite charming, my dear,' Isabella said
warmly as they reached her side, patting the chair to the
left of her as she spoke.

'Thank you.' Fabia looked into the wrinkled old face
warily. She had the distinct impression that those bright
black button eyes saw far more than Isabella revealed.

'I like to have young people around me,' Isabella said
comfortably as John began serving the soup from a large
silver tureen. 'Makes me feel young. Too many old fogies
in this house, eh, John?' She smiled wickedly at the
elderly butler, whose face remained in its impassive lines.

'As you say, madam,' he replied blandly.

Isabella gave a cackle of laughter as she turned again
to Fabia. 'He thinks I'm a dreadful old lady,' she said
with a wave of her hand at John. 'Quite dreadful. Isn't
that right, John?'

'As you say, madam,' he said again, his face dead-
pan, but as the old man's eyes met those of his mistress
over the soup tureen Fabia saw a smile in their watery
blueness that matched a light in Isabella's. The two
understood each other, she realised suddenly, perfectly.

'How long have you known my grandson, Fabia?'
Isabella asked after a few minutes of silence.

'Just a few weeks.' Fabia had practised this little speech
in her head for so long it came out quite naturally. 'We
met at a social function Alex was holding. My friend
and I had been given tickets at the last moment and we
thought it was a shame to waste them.'

'Another of your charity dos, Alexander?' Isabella asked disapprovingly. Alex nodded without speaking and his grandmother turned to Fabia again, her lined face irritable. 'I keep telling him, he's too busy to bother with such things, he works all hours of the day and night as it is. Work, work, work...' She eyed her grandson morosely. 'But he says just giving a donation himself is not enough, that other people's consciences need to be awakened, those who can afford it, that is.' She looked at Fabia sharply. 'What do you think?'

The abrupt question, coming on top of the surprising revelations that Alex worked too hard and actually cared about the charities he supported, temporarily robbed Fabia of speech and she stared at Isabella for a second, her mouth opening and then closing.

'I think Fabia would like to eat her dinner in peace,' Alex said smoothly, meeting her eyes for a split-second over the dining-table. 'All right, Grandmama?' His tone was mild but there was a touch of steel in the softness that the old woman clearly recognised.

'So I'm talking too much, so what's new?' Fabia had a sudden urge to giggle but restrained it with difficulty. This irascible old woman was outrageous but she liked her brand of unpretentious honesty and uncompromising veracity. There was an integrity about Isabella that was unmistakable, very much like her grandson—she caught her thoughts sharply. No, she hadn't thought that, she *wouldn't* be fooled again.

As the meal progressed she found that playing the part allotted to her became more and more difficult, due mainly to the close proximity of Alex rather than anything else. He reached across the table a couple of times, taking her hand briefly in a little show of affection that had her wanting to snatch it back at once. She didn't like the feel of his hard warm flesh on hers; it was...unsettling. Added to which those sharp bird-like eyes of his grandmother seemed to be watching her every move. She forced her mouth to smile, talked lightly of this and that, but had the distinct impression that she wasn't fooling Isabella for a second. The old woman knew there was something wrong, she just didn't know what it was—for the moment.

Yet the old lady seemed to like her. As Fabia talked frankly about her humble beginnings, her job, the little flat that she called home, she sensed she had gained Isabella's friendship. Isabella became quite animated at one point, reminiscing about her equally modest childhood as the youngest daughter of a poor Italian family in a little obscure village deep in the countryside of rural Italy. 'Then Henry comes along one day,' she said dreamily, 'Alexander's grandfather. His parents had sent him to do a tour of Europe; they still did it in those days.' She nodded to herself. 'And he couldn't speak a word of Italian and I knew no English. But we communicated.' She raised dark eyes to Fabia's interested gaze. 'In a manner as old as time.' Alexander shifted uneasily but the old lady was not going to be silenced this time. 'When Henry wanted to marry me his parents were horrified, and mine...' She laughed softly. 'They dragged me off to the priest and asked him to keep me locked in a room at the church. It was shameful, you see; I was a Catholic Italian girl and he was English and not of the same religion.'

'What did you do?' asked Fabia, fascinated.

'Alexander will tell you, won't you, my dear?' Isabella sank back in her chair. 'I'm tired.'

'Oh, it doesn't matter, please, leave it if——' The old lady interrupted her forcibly, waving her hands at Fabia irritably, her strong voice belying the excuse of exhaustion.

'Alexander knows the tale, he's heard it often enough. Tell Fabia what happened, my boy.' Fabia looked keenly into the dried-up old face. For some reason known only to herself Isabella wanted Alex to tell her the rest of the story.

'If you insist,' Alex said lazily, his flecked eyes with their strange golden light fastening on Fabia's pale, beautiful face tightly. 'My grandfather was determined to have her; he would listen to no one. Late one night he got a ladder and rescued her from the church. They eloped. For a time both sets of families would have nothing to do with them but then my father was born and...babies have a way of smoothing family feuds out.' He paused, his darkly tanned face and long thick burnished hair giving him the aura of a fierce brigand in the dim light from the shaded standard lamps, one at each end of the room. 'He had to have her, you see. Once he had found her there was no way on earth anyone would have persuaded him to let her go. He would have died first.' There was an emotion in his voice that had her transfixed now, her eyes locked with his, her head refusing to accept the message her heart was giving her as she looked into his waiting face. 'There's an old story about the Cade men; it goes on from generation to generation. We only love once, just once in our lives, but when we do it's for eternity.'

'Is it true?' she whispered breathlessly, mesmerised by the atmosphere that had thickened like a powerful drug.

'Oh, yes.' His eyes were burning into her. 'Quite true.'

Isabella expelled a satisfied sigh, nodding her head like a wise old owl. 'So now you know, my dear.' She looked hard at Fabia. 'Don't you?' There seemed to be more in the question than its face value and Fabia stared at her silently, trying to read the razor-sharp mind behind those bright black eyes.

'Yes, of course, thank you for telling me your story,' she said carefully, fighting the urge to lift her gaze to Alex's and see what was written in the hard face, afraid of what she might see. Laughter? Mockery? Scorn? He was sitting as still as a statue and she was vitally conscious of every line of his body as though she were looking at him.

She wondered what he *really* thought of the old story. He would have had to agree with it in front of his grandmother, knowing it meant so much to her, but what of him, and all those countless women he had known?

The rest of the evening passed pleasantly enough and when Isabella retired for bed, at just after ten, Fabia waited until the old lady had disappeared with the ever faithful John at her side, it being Christine's half-day off, and then made her escape from Alex's sombre presence. He nodded slowly at her hesitant 'goodnight', his dark face enigmatically distant, but she was conscious of his eyes on her as she climbed the long curving staircase, their heat burning into her back as though their light came from the sun itself. She glanced round just before disappearing from view to find his gaze tightly fixed on her as she had expected, the big body taut and still, the goblet of brandy in his left hand motionless. Everything in his stance suggested an attitude of waiting and it unnerved her without reason; she didn't understand him and she understood herself still less.

Later, in the soft downy warmth of the huge double bed, she cried for the first time in years, long racking sobs that did nothing to ease the ache inside her, the sense of loss and despair that had grown all day.

I'm just tired, tired and nervous, she told herself firmly when the worst of the weeping had passed. I'm in an unfamiliar environment, an alien in a different, fabulously seductive world where I don't know the rules and I'm surrounded by strangers who talk in riddles and expect me to understand. She bounced her head in agreement with herself.

She'd be different in the morning. In the cold clear light of day all the forgotten dreams and hopes that a certain six-foot-four, tawny-eyed stranger had resurrected would sink back to their rightful place, buried deep in the hidden recesses of her mind, locked away from prying eyes.

'I *am* happy,' she whispered defiantly into the beautiful empty room. 'No one has everything they want, after all.' She was a career girl now, a totally different creature from the childlike romantic whom Robin had picked up and discarded so brutally. And she wanted it that way. *She did*!

CHAPTER SIX

'IT'S beautiful, Alex.' Fabia stood awe-struck in the doorway of the main drawing-room, her eyes wide with wonder as she looked up at the magnificent seven-foot tree towering above her, its sweet-smelling pine branches covered in red ribbon, glittering white stars and small delicately formed candles in red and white twists. 'I've never seen such a gorgeous tree.'

'I get one each year for Isabella,' Alex said quietly as his eyes stroked her glowing face, a warmth in their gold depths that caused her breath to shudder in her throat. 'In Italy, when she was a child, each house couldn't afford a tree with decorations and presents so all the villagers would get together and bring a tree down from the mountainside for the village square. I know the story by heart and you'll be hearing it soon, no doubt.' He smiled slowly. 'Each family would give what trimming they could, a ribbon there, an ornament here; she pines for those times now she's alone.'

'She has you,' she said softly, meeting his gaze, before her eyes were drawn to the mass of gaily wrapped parcels piled around the huge terracotta pot filled with earth in which the tree's roots were embedded.

'Isabella assures me the adults made sure even the poorest child had a gift on the Saviour's birthday. There aren't too many barefoot little ragamuffins round here but we donate the presents to the children's ward at the hospital on Christmas Eve.' He shrugged lightly. 'It's become something of a tradition.'

'I think that's lovely.' She smiled up into his watching eyes and for a moment he looked as though he was going to say more, but then he turned away dismissively.

'I have my moments of weakness,' he drawled with mocking sarcasm, and she flushed at the taunting note in his voice. She had woken that morning deep in the luxurious warmth of the big bed and decided that the only way she was going to get through the next week was to take each day as it came. No more heart-searching, no more dissecting things that were better left alone. She was nothing to Alex, she had to remember that; he could have as many girlfriends as he liked, it was *absolutely* nothing to do with her. He was used to sophisticated worldly women to whom love-affairs were merely pleasant diversions for a limited time. She knew that...so why did the picture of a tall dark-haired woman with pouting red lips keep flashing into her mind in taunting ridicule?

They ate alone in the large breakfast-room—Isabella never rose before lunchtime—and just as they finished the doorbell rang. The morning was filled with visits from friends and relations and several of the women, Fabia noticed wryly, put great enthusiasm into greeting Alex. He remained his normal charming self, acting his part magnificently as he drew Fabia to his side time and time again, dropping a kiss on her fair head or hugging her close in a swift embrace. 'You don't need to keep doing that,' she whispered angrily after one long unexpected kiss on the lips, emerging flushed and breathless with a strange little tremor in her stomach.

'I like it,' he murmured unrepentantly in her ear, his warm breath causing her to shudder helplessly. 'Don't you?'

'No, I do not,' she snapped back quickly, all the finer feelings of the morning melting into hot rage. 'I'm here acting as your girlfriend, not your...your——'

'But I kiss my girlfriends, angel-face; I kiss them a lot,' Alex said softly with his eyes tight on her pink face. She could hear a thread of amusement in the deep voice and longed to slap the cool, handsome face, hard! 'Don't the men in your life like to express their appreciation of your finer qualities?'

She glared at him ferociously and spoke without thinking, provoked by his cynical mockery. 'I don't have any——' She stopped abruptly as his eyes narrowed into gold slits. 'I mean...' She paused again, searching for the right words that wouldn't betray her.

'What *do* you mean, Fabia?' There was no trace of amusement or mockery in the hard face now, more a slightly incredulous intentness that totally unnerved her. 'Are you seriously telling me——?'

'I'm not telling you anything,' she said bitterly as she jerked away from his side, walking over to the other side of the crowded room without turning round. How could she have been so stupid as to let that little snippet of news slip? Maybe he would assume she had meant there was no one special at the moment? The hope died as it was born. No, he was too astute by half. She had unwittingly divulged her chaste state and to a man like him it would be like the ultimate challenge. Damn, damn, damn! She was making a real mess of all this.

It was as they all walked through to the dining-room for a buffet-style lunch and Fabia caught a glimpse of yet more presents piled high on one of the occasional tables in the hall that the dreadful realisation dawned on her. She hadn't brought any presents! She stopped so that Alex, a step behind her, cannoned into her back, his arms going out to hold her as she stumbled forwards. 'Very nice, but what's the matter?' he said softly as he caught sight of her stricken face.

'I didn't bring any presents, Alex.' She stared up at him in horror. 'How could I have forgotten? I should have got your grandmother something, I just wasn't thinking straight. What shall I do?' She glanced round helplessly.

'Don't look so tragic.' He smiled at her consternation, his voice wry. 'It's Christmas Eve, remember? The shops will stay open until they've extracted the last penny from the happy public who wander around in a daze of goodwill and whisky.' She didn't like the cynicism and turned away sharply, her face expressing her feelings more adequately than words.

'Sorry.' He turned her to him again and this time his face was clear of all sarcasm. 'I'll take you into town when we've had lunch,' he said quietly. 'You can do your shopping there.'

'No, I don't want to take you away from all your guests,' she said quickly with a little gesture of repudiation. 'You stay here—I'll call a taxi.'

'No need.' His voice was tight. 'It's open house here on Christmas Eve, everyone knows that. People just come and go as they please. I'll take you.'

'No, really.' She suddenly couldn't face the thought of being close to him again in the car, those long muscled legs stretched out so close to hers and the subtle, distinctly male smell of him filling the air round her with sensual promise. 'You stay here—your grandmother——'

'For crying out loud, woman!' He swung her round so quickly as she made to turn away that her head snapped on her shoulders, her hair flying over her face in silken disarray. 'Can't you bear my company for as short a time as that? Am I really so obnoxious to you?' She stared at him as he glared down at her, his face as black as thunder. 'I'm trying, I'm really trying to keep my temper with you, Fabia, but you know how to push a man to the limit, don't you? Now whether you like it or not I'm going to take you into the damn town.

Another word and so help me I won't be responsible for my reactions.' After one more furious scowl he walked past her into the gaiety beyond, leaving her standing shaking and silent in the deserted hall.

This was ridiculous; he had no right to talk to her like that, she thought angrily as she smoothed the soft woollen dress she was wearing over her hips with shaking hands and flung back the thick gold hair from her face. She wasn't going to fall at his feet in gratitude for his company whatever the other women did. A vision of clinging arms round his neck and a bright red mouth close to his made her wince with sudden pain. He was arrogant and overbearing and everything she disliked in a man, and if he couldn't take the way she felt about him he should let her go home, where she belonged.

The air was bitingly cold and crystal-clear as they left the warm brightness of the house some time later. A weak yellow sun lit the white snow into blinding silver, the stark black branches of the bare trees standing out against the pale hoary sky in vivid contrast. She stood for a moment at the top of the steps as Alex walked past her to the car parked below and drew deeply on the fragrant icy air, shutting her eyes as she let its cold clear breath stir her lungs. After the close warmth of the house it felt wonderfully good.

It was a beautiful winter's day and it was Christmas Eve, she thought suddenly, and life was good. Whatever, life was good.

'You look like the spirit of winter with your head back like that and the sun on your hair,' Alex said gruffly, and as she opened her eyes and caught the full force of his golden gaze she stood transfixed for a long moment, caught by the magic of the moment. 'Come on, you'll get cold.' He broke the spell abruptly, turning away with a brusque nod of his head, his voice terse and his body stiff as though he was holding himself in control.

'This is a beautiful car.' She ran her hand down the smooth red paint of the Ferrari as she sank down into the soft leather seat. 'It isn't the one we came in, is it?'

'No, I have several cars,' he said shortly, his face cold as though she had said the words in criticism. She glanced at him as he shut her door and strode round the car to the driving side. He looked bad-tempered and angry, and undeniably gorgeous. She caught herself quickly. None of that, Fabia, she said silently to that other self she seemed to be talking to a lot recently. He's your employer and this is a temporary job, nothing else. Concentrate on that and that only.

It would have been a short journey into the town in normal conditions but due to the thick snow blanketing the countryside the powerful car was forced to crawl along, nosing its way through the space cleared in the middle of the main roads, which were narrow enough at the best of times. The wooded hills rolling southwards were frozen in pale silent beauty, sheltered farms and hamlets motionless except for thin spirals of smoke rising from weathered chimneys.

They made the journey in almost total silence and, although she tried to concentrate on the beauty of the countryside in its mantle of bridal white, her thoughts were drawn back time and time again to the dark-haired woman who had flung her arms round his neck with such familiarity. How many women had he known? How many did he still know? She bit her lip silently. He wasn't the sort of man to be without female companionship too long. No doubt he was in the middle of some sort of liaison right now. He had said that there were several women he could have asked to spend Christmas with him except that all of them would prove difficult to unload once the holiday was over. She glanced at him under her lashes, the strong firm hands that she knew by experience could be devastatingly gentle, the hard powerful body so vitally male——

'Would you like me to come in with you?'

As his voice jerked her out of her perusal she glanced out of the window and saw they were just entering the town, an enchanting little maze of narrow streets, snug squares and brightly lit low-tiled shops, timelessly picturesque under the snow-filled white sky. 'Sorry?'

'The shops. Would you like me to come with you?' he repeated patiently, easing the car along slowly in the nose-to-tail traffic, the packed pavements on either side of the narrow street threatening to thrust their burden of scurrying humans into their path at every turn.

'Not if you've something else to do,' she said quickly and then caught his sigh of exasperation as he drew into the 'reserved' space in a bulgingly full car park outside a large store.

'Does that mean yes or no?' he asked drily as he cut the ignition with a small sigh. 'Translate for me.'

'Well, I suppose I might get lost,' she said carefully, and after one searing glance he stretched lazily before opening his door.

'I've had sweeter offers but that will have to do,' he said with heavy sarcasm as he walked round the car and opened her door. 'I think I realised very early on in our acquaintance that as an ego-booster you were a non-starter.'

'I wouldn't have thought you of all people would need one,' she said quickly as she climbed out of the car, his hand on her arm.

'Oh, yes?' he said mildly but with a faint narrowing of the cat-like eyes. 'And why is that?' He turned her to face him, tucking her collar up round her neck as though she were a child and kissing the tip of her nose with warm lips.

The unexpected tenderness took her completely by surprise and she stared at him stupidly for a moment, her violet eyes with their heavy fringe of lashes wide with confusion.

'Why is that?' he repeated softly, tilting her chin up to him with one finger and drawing her against him so that she was tight within the circle of his arm. 'Tell me.'

'You're so...' Her voice trailed away as he kissed the tip of her nose again. 'Don't do that, I've told you.'

'You've told me a lot of things, angel-face,' he said comfortably as he tucked her arm in his and led her towards the shop. 'Whether I'm prepared to listen to them is another story, of course.' She tried to wrench her arm from his but his grip tightened until she was forced to give in.

'Mr Cade, how nice to see you, sir.' They had only been in the hot perfumed atmosphere of the shop for sixty seconds when a smartly dressed little man in a pin-striped suit came hurrying over to Alex's side, his jowls bobbing with delight. 'We've kept your space in the car park free for the last few days, sir, in case you decided to shop with us. I hope it was available for you?'

'Yes, it was clear, thank you.' Alex smiled dismissively, and after a long curious look at Fabia the small man backed away carefully, his head still nodding ingratiatingly, in much the same way that the common herd left the presence of a king in days gone by.

'What was all that about?' Fabia asked, stopping to look up into Alex's closed face. 'Who's that man?'

'The manager of this store,' Alex replied shortly. 'Now shall we——?'

She ignored the proffered hand and remained where she was. 'That space in the car park—is it kept specially for you, then, always?'

'Yes.' He looked down at her quietly. 'It is.'

'Why?' She stared up at him, noticing as she did so, in a strangely detached sort of way, that he was head and shoulders above any other of the men milling round them in the crowded store, his tanned skin and tawny colouring accentuated by the lights overhead.

'Because I own this building.' A dry smile twisted his lips. 'Another nail in my coffin?'

'You own it?' She glanced round the fabulously elegant store in amazement.

'I own the whole block,' he said slowly with a resigned expression on his face, 'and I'm blowed if I know why I'm trying to keep it from you except that it places a few more bricks in place, doesn't it?'

'Bricks?' This conversation was becoming more bizarre each moment.

'Yes, bricks,' he said shortly. 'As in "building", you know, like the ones you use so well in the construction of this wall to stop me getting inside that strange little head of yours.'

'I don't know what you're talking about,' she said shakily. The hard golden glare was unnerving.

'No?' He smiled coldly. 'I think you do. I think you know exactly what I mean, Fabia, and for the record——'

'Alex, darling...' As an overdressed, gushing matron of considerable years caught his arm Fabia made her escape.

'I'll be back here in ten minutes,' she muttered shortly and, ignoring his call, dived into the mêlée quickly, avoiding his restraining hand with a turn of her body as she went. She fought her way over to a relatively clear space beside a massive Christmas tree and stood for a moment, more shaken than she cared to admit. What did he mean when he said things like that? It was almost as though he cared, really cared about her opinion of him. She shook herself. Stop it, she thought grimly, you're trying to believe what you want to believe. Of course he'd like to get under your skin—for a time. Once you'd served your purpose it would be 'bye bye, Fabia' without a second thought. Wake up, girl!

Taking the lift up to the next floor, she wandered about for five minutes wondering what on earth she could buy a woman of eighty-seven who had everything she wanted and had for the last sixty-five years! The ten minutes were nearly up when she noticed a display of gaily worked tapestry blankets in a corner, and, remembering the heavy blanket wrapped round Isabella's legs on their first meeting, she decided that would do. It was ridiculously expensive but she bought it anyway and was just standing waiting for the lift to take her down to the ground floor again when she spied a tiny hoop of silver key-rings on the cosmetics counter. Each one had a minute mirror attached to it, and as she stood looking at them she made up her mind. He would see the joke, wouldn't he?

'Would you like me to gift-wrap it for you?' The tall, beautifully dressed willowy blonde was all long red-painted nails and flashing gold bracelets as she carefully placed the small key-ring in a tiny box and wrapped it with a small white bow, fixing a little card to the outside and handing Fabia a pen.

'Oh…thank you.' She thought for a moment and then wrote swiftly, 'Who caught who?' Would he tie it in with that first message?

Alex was standing just where she had left him when she stepped out of the lift and as she glanced over and saw his big dark figure quite detached from the rest of the noisy milling throng she felt a jolting sensation in her heart region. He looked severe and distant, and absolutely gorgeous.

The golden gaze fixed on her when she was a few yards away and he smiled lazily, his eyes travelling to the huge box in her hands which contained Isabella's gift. The key-ring was in her pocket. 'You don't mean to say you've chosen something already?' he said mockingly as she reached his side. '"Curiouser and curiouser", as Lewis Carroll wrote. You're a real little Alice, aren't you?'

'Am I?' She smiled nonchalantly, her stomach churning as he wrapped an arm protectively round her shoulders, pulling her into his side, fighting the pleasure the act of possession aroused.

'You sure are.' He looked down at her, his eyes travelling over the tousled blonde hair and huge violet eyes before they fastened on her lips. There was a heat in their depths that caused the fluttering in her stomach to intensify a hundredfold. 'Most of the women I know take a couple of hours to choose a lipstick!'

'Do they?' She smiled again, forcing her lips to turn upwards as his words rang painfully in her ears. 'Most of the women I know'. Oh, she hated all this, she did!

'Fancy a coffee before we leave?' He took the box from her, tucking it under his arm.

'Where?' They were moving towards the lift and he glanced down at her, a wry smile on his face.

'Well, we could go to my office on the top floor. It's nice and warm there and quite secluded, and once Tomkins has brought the coffee I could make sure we are quite alone. Or...' the tawny gaze was mocking '...we could go to the coffee lounge on the third floor.'

They stepped into the lift and he smiled down at her pink face as he pressed the button for the third floor. 'When I think of the girls who would have jumped at that offer,' he said lazily into her ear as they stood pressed together in the close confines of the crowded lift. 'You don't know what you're missing.'

'Why don't you ask one of them, then?' she said snappily as the metal doors swished open on the third floor.

His answering chuckle made her teeth grind in helpless defiance and she eyed him balefully as he led her over to the fresh aroma of percolating coffee.

It was dusk when they stepped back into the icy air, the pavements treacherous underfoot and the heavy sky a pale pink against the white world beneath. The long, low car was forced to pick its way carefully through the crowded streets, growling softly at the indignity, and then they were in the open countryside again, the hedges and trees picked out in startling clarity against the darkening red sky.

'There's a picture-book view at the top of this hill,' Alex said quietly when they had been driving for ten minutes or so. As they reached the peak of the gently rising fell he drew to a halt, letting the slow purr of the car's engine fall silent as the grandeur of the sweeping wooded slopes dotted with the odd stone farmhouse and tiny isolated village tucked away in the snow-covered expanse worked their timeless magic.

Fabia forgot the flutter of panic she had felt when he had stopped the car, forgot that the man sitting next to her so quietly was a ruthless man of the world used to having his smallest whim granted with immediate deference, forgot everything as she gazed out into the miles upon miles of Christmas-card countryside frozen in exquisitely pale beauty beneath a darkening sky of red and gold. It was breathtaking, and the heavens had turned a light milky grey before she glanced at him, coming back to the world surrounding her with a small sigh that expressed what words couldn't.

His eyes were fixed tight on her face, a sensual slumberous warmth in their browny-gold depths that had her breath catching in her throat and her lips half opening in anticipation. His mouth was warm and mobile as it covered hers demandingly until he was crouched over her in her seat and she felt as if time itself had been suspended. His hands moved beneath the warm tweed of her coat without her realising it, drawing her into him with sensuous ease as they caressed each curve and contour of her melting body. She was utterly lost in the moment, the beauty of the world outside and the scent of his light tangy aftershave creating a heady sensation of pliant, soft oneness that had her moaning his name against his hard mouth. His breathing was harsh and ragged as he felt her response and now his lips were exploring her face as though he were blind, moving over her flushed skin in tiny darting kisses that had her straining against him for more, her arms reaching up to the broad shoulders above her in wordless abandonment.

It was when she felt the coolness of air tighten her breasts that realisation dawned. She had been unaware that he had unbuttoned her dress, unaware of anything except the sweet pressure of his mouth and the feel of the hard, dominant body next to hers, but now she recoiled as though he had struck her, moving violently beneath him so that his hands were stilled and his mouth raised from hers.

'What is it?' He raised his head to stare into the wide, shocked blue eyes. 'I won't hurt you—don't be frightened.'

'No...' She struggled against him, pushing his hard chest with the flat of her hands, and he moved away immediately, his face settling into the expressionless mould she knew so well that hid his feelings like a cold blank mask.

'It's him, isn't it,' he said quietly and with no trace of emotion in his voice, making the words a statement rather than a question. 'It might be over but you're still thinking of him, aren't you?' The slanted eyes swept over her flushed face as he raked back his heavy fall of hair with his fingers. 'Do you love him that much? He must have left you, finished it, and yet you still want him that badly?' As he turned from her and rested his hands on the steering-wheel she noticed, with a detached numbness, that they were shaking slightly, but apart from that he betrayed no feeling at all. They could have been discussing the weather all those moments before, such was the quietness of his whole being now.

'I can't explain...' She knew she was going to cry in another moment and bit hard on her bottom lip to still the tears as she buttoned her dress with shaking hands, staring out of the side-window into the colourless world outside as she pulled her coat more closely round her.

After a full minute he relaxed back into his seat with a deep sigh, his hands still on the steering-wheel and his eyes straight ahead. 'I'm sorry, Fabia; believe it or not, that wasn't planned,' he said quietly. 'I'm not the sort of man to seize upon any advantage and it's been years since I've made love in a car.' He stopped suddenly. 'Hell, I'm making things worse, aren't I? What I'm trying to say is——'

'I know, I know.' She couldn't look at him—if she did she would be lost—so she stared out through the side-window, her face as white as the snow outside. 'Could we go back now, please...?'

He said nothing, adjusting his long legs in the close confines of the car as he turned the key in the ignition, his face grim and cold as he checked the mirrors before turning the car fully into the road and continuing down the hill, the car lights gleaming yellow in the darkness.

She felt sick with mounting horror as she remembered how easily he had overcome all the barriers erected so firmly during the last seven years. She had barely allowed a man to kiss her in all that time, earning a reputation for frigidity, she knew, but hugging it to her as though it were a prize. She hadn't wanted to be involved with anyone again—even the nicest of the men she had occasionally dated had left her cold—and here she had virtually thrown herself into his arms, inviting—— She closed her eyes for a second and forced back the tears that were threatening to overflow. Inviting a lot more than she had got, she admitted honestly. She couldn't have blamed him if he had been unable to stop; all her signals had been bright green . . . She moaned silently. What was he thinking? She dared not risk a glance at his face.

The short drive home seemed like hours, so rigid and tense was her body, and as they drove through the gates and into the sweep of the long drive she uncurled her hands from her lap and tried to soften the tightness in her face. It was Christmas Eve, there was bound to be a houseful when they got in, and she had to appear relatively normal if only for Isabella's sake.

It seemed as though every light in the house was glaring as they drew to a scrunchy halt outside the door, and as Alex noticed a large white Mercedes to one side of the driveway he frowned, his eyes narrowing in protest. 'Great, just what we need—Susan and family *en masse*, if I'm not mistaken. I told everyone to keep their visits confined to the day for once; Isabella can't take too much excitement and she'll be exhausted by now.'

'Susan?' Her timid enquiry was lost as he opened his door abruptly and marched round to her side of the car, opening her door and helping her out with his eyes fixed on the house. Almost as though he had willed it, the door opened a second later to reveal a horribly familiar figure, the sleek dark hair swept up into an elegant chignon, each strand beautifully in place.

'Alex, darling, we've been waiting absolutely ages. We couldn't go without saying hello, now, could we?' The woman moved gracefully towards them down the steps, and as she placed herself unasked into Alex's arms Fabia realised she was a little older than she had first supposed, probably thirty or so, and as the lovely face glanced at her for a piercing moment with big beautiful green eyes Fabia knew something akin to an electric shock shoot down her spine. She had never before in her life experienced a look of such angry, undisguised hate; there had been something in those jade-green eyes that was positively malignant, something that reached out at her through the icy air with fierce animal viciousness and curled her insides in protest.

'Susan.' Alex gently disentangled the slim arms from around his neck and placed them firmly at the woman's sides, softening the gesture with a warm smile as he looked down at the beautiful face staring up at him. 'Are your parents with you, and the children?'

'Of course.' Seemingly unrebuffed, Susan placed her arm in his, ignoring Fabia as though she didn't exist. 'Daddy had to drive. You know I daren't take the car out on roads like these.' She smiled helplessly up into his face like a little girl asking for approval.

'I'd like you to meet Fabia.' He uncoiled Susan's arm with amazing dexterity and reached out for Fabia, curving her into the crook of his arm as he moved slightly to one side. 'Fabia, meet Susan, an old friend of the family.'

'Hello.' Fabia smiled into the beautifully made-up face, noticing as she did so that Susan's large green eyes had turned glacial the moment they had fixed on her.

'Hello, sweetie.' Susan held out a soft manicured white hand. 'I've seen you before, haven't I, at one of Alex's receptions?' She smiled a sugar-sweet smile that didn't reach the cold jade eyes. 'I didn't realise you were one of Alex's . . . girlfriends.'

The brief but very definite hesitation before the word 'girlfriend' was a subtle insult that only another woman would recognise, and Fabia looked hard at the other woman, her face straight. 'Probably because I'm not *one* of them,' she said coolly. 'I've never been one for sharing what belongs to me. I am *the* girlfriend.' She smiled a slow, long deliberate smile.

Both Susan and Alex were staring at her with equal astonishment on their faces if for different reasons. Alex clearly had no idea why Fabia had stated her case so firmly and Susan was obviously astounded that the gauntlet had been taken up with such speed. She opened her mouth to say more and then caught the glint in Fabia's eye and decided against it. 'How nice...'

Fabia smiled sweetly. 'We think so, don't we, darling?' She looked up into Alex's face, which had a distinctly mesmerised tinge to it now. He had said he wanted her to be herself, hadn't he? Well, there was no way she was going to let a spoilt little rich girl like Susan put her down without a fight.

'Uncle Alex! Uncle Alex!' As two small figures came hurtling through the open doorway and launched themselves into Alex's arms she caught an expression of what could almost be termed triumph on Susan's face. What now? It was clear the children adored him and he them, and as Fabia walked by Alex's side into the house, a child perched on each of his arms, she wondered with a feeling of dread gripping her heart what other little surprises Alex had in store for her this Christmas.

CHAPTER SEVEN

BY THE time Susan's parents left an hour later with their daughter and grandchildren in tow, Fabia had passed through so many different emotions that she felt quite exhausted. The initial feeling of outrage at the other woman's deliberate snub and continued offhand disregard that bordered on rudeness had first changed to exasperation, then contemptuous disgust, to finish in such a mixture of feelings that even she couldn't have named them. Apart from one—anger. That alone had remained constant throughout.

The instinctive dislike that had first risen with Susan's discourtesy had been swiftly replaced by revulsion at the way the other woman quite blatantly used her children to further her friendship with Alex, encouraging them to sit on his knee and exulting openly in his easy relationship with them. 'Isn't Alex just a darling with the kiddies?' Susan said in a soft undertone to Fabia as she was preparing to leave. 'I just don't like to think how I would have coped without him when poor William died.'

'William?' Fabia asked coolly.

'My late husband, such a dear, dear man,' Susan said unemotionally. 'Heaps older than me, of course, but he was so in love with me and I was too young then to know what I really wanted.' The hard green eyes fastened on Alex hungrily.

'But of course you are quite a few years older now?' Fabia said drily, deciding enough was enough, and effectively finishing further conversation as Susan departed with head held high and cheeks burning, her eyes glacial.

Alex seemed to take an inordinate amount of time seeing them all off and his smile as he re-entered the room seemed like the last straw. 'Anything wrong, Fabia?' He looked at her oddly.

'Fabia has a headache,' Isabella intervened firmly and smoothly with an understanding glance at her stiff face. 'Why don't you go and have a rest before dinner, Fabia? I intend to.'

Those sharp black eyes missed very little, Fabia thought wryly as she smiled gratefully at Isabella. The tiny woman had been aware of every little subtle snub Susan had sent in her direction and Fabia had noticed Isabella's coldness with the lovely brunette. 'I will, thank you,' she said quietly, leaving the room quickly with just a cool nod at Alex as she passed him. The fact that he appeared quite oblivious both to Susan's behaviour and her own fury made her doubly irritated as she lay down on the soft bed, turning out the main light and leaving just the subdued glow from one small lamp to light the large room.

Men can be so blind, she thought bitterly as she lay in the warm semi-darkness, her mind buzzing with a thousand images. Alex chasing Gemma, Susan's little five-year-old, on all fours, growling madly while pretending to be a lion. Alex listening seriously with complete concentration while Jeremy, at eight years old, explained the rudiments of football. Alex—— 'Stop it, stop it!' Her voice was loud in the empty room and she rolled over on the bed, hands on her ears as she endeavoured to shut out the pictures.

It had hurt to see him like that and she didn't understand why. She could cope with the ruthless millionaire businessman image or charming philanderer—just—but seeing him playing with the children, his male strength more marked against their fragility, had touched some-thing deep inside her that was acutely painful.

He's nothing to you, so it doesn't matter, she told herself firmly as she glanced at her watch, deciding to have a leisurely bath before dinner. Susan isn't the first and she won't be the last, you know that. *You know it.*

So why, when she knew the inescapable truth, did it hurt so much? she thought later as she lay soaking in the warm, scented water. Why was there a permanent ache in her heart these days, and why the mad churning in her stomach every time she so much as thought of him?

I wish I could go back to the flat, she thought sud-denly. Back to a safe little hidey-hole where I could lick my wounds in peace. But I haven't got any wounds, she argued hotly with that voice in her mind, sitting bolt upright in the bubbles, slopping water over the edge of the bath on to the thick fluffy carpet. I won't let there be any!

She heard the knock on the door and tensed before remembering that it was Mary's time to come and turn down the beds, a ritual she never missed and insisted on doing. The small woman had taken to spending five minutes with her when possible, filling her in on the history of the house and its occupants.

'Come in...' She slid back down under the bubbles as she spoke.

'Now I'd love to take you up on that, I really would, but as I suspect the invitation was given in error I'll re-strain my natural tendencies with noble self-control.'

'Alex?' Her voice was a panic-stricken squeak. 'I thought you were Mary. *Don't* come in!'

The sound of a lazy rich chuckle did amazing things to her insides and she curled her toes in the water, her heart jumping. 'You really haven't got the spirit of Christmas at all, angel-face—goodwill to all men and so on.' There was a moment's silence and when she didn't speak he tapped the door again gently. 'I just called by to say that Isabella is feeling rather tired and is going to have dinner in her room.' There was a faint note of concern for his grandmother in the dark voice in spite of his efforts to hide it. 'It will just be the two of us downstairs so don't bother to dress for dinner—we'll be relaxed and casual. OK?'

She knew what he meant but a sudden vision of them both sitting at the magnificent dining-table stark naked brought a smile to her lips and hot colour to her cheeks. Where had that thought come from? 'OK, see you in a minute,' she said reluctantly, suddenly realising that without Isabella's presence the meal would become subtly more intimate.

She dressed simply in a plain blue dress that perfectly matched the colour of her eyes, adding tiny gold studs to her ears and a small dab of perfume to her wrists. She debated on whether to put her hair up but a tiny nagging memory of a long white neck and gleaming black hair coiled perfectly in place decided her against it. She would not lower herself to compete for a prize she had no intention of claiming anyway!

He was sitting in one of the easy-chairs at the bottom of the curving staircase as she made her way downstairs, rising instantly he heard her approach, his hard handsome face unreadable. 'You look lovely, Fabia,' he said softly. 'One can't improve on perfection but perhaps you'd like to wear this anyway.' He handed her a small transparent box through which the creamy furled petals of an exotic orchid were visible.

'Oh, it's beautiful, Alex.' She looked up into his face in delight, the flawless purity of the hothouse flower touching something deep inside her.

'They had more brilliant colours and shapes but that one seemed right for you.' He took the bloom out of its box and she saw that the petals were veined with faint blue and gold towards the centre of the flower, culminating in a deep vibrant violet at its heart. 'The correct name is unpronounceable but it's known as "unawakened",' he said blandly as he fixed the orchid carefully on her dress, his hands accidentally brushing the side of her breast as he did so and causing a deep heat to rise in her flesh. He seemed quite oblivious to her agitation, taking a strand of long corn-coloured hair in his fingers and letting the smooth silk slip through them as he finished.

'Thank you.' She stepped back a pace as she spoke, her hand nervously touching the flower as she stared, unsmiling now, into the sombre darkness of his face. He had discarded the formal dinner-jacket he usually wore for light trousers and a pale Aran sweater, the cream of the wool throwing his tanned skin and rich brown hair into stark contrast, and somehow emphasising his great height. He looked powerful and dangerous and irresistibly attractive and the blood drummed crazily in her ears as he took her hand and led her into the dimly lit dining-room.

The table was beautifully decorated in Christmas colours of red and green, the glittering silver cutlery and fine crystal glassware enriched with looped scrolled ribbons and sprays of holly, the centrepiece a magnificent arrangement of sweet-smelling deep red roses, red and green ribbon and soft feathery fern.

'Mary does tend to go overboard at Christmas,' Alex said drily as he pulled out the chair for her to sit down. 'Would you like a sherry or a glass of wine before we eat? Dinner will be promptly served in exactly,' he consulted the heavy gold watch on his wrist, 'eight minutes if I know anything about this household.'

'A sherry, please.' She was feeling distinctly uncomfortable and painfully shy and both sensations made her jumpy. He seemed different tonight somehow, although she didn't know why. She was just conscious of the fact that every inflexion of his voice, every little movement he made, registered on her taut nerves like an electric shock.

As he placed the glass of sherry in her hand he slipped a long gold package on the table at the side of her fork. 'Merry Christmas.' She raised startled eyes to find him looking down at her with that strange expression on his face she had seen once or twice before and once again it was swiftly veiled as he caught her glance.

'What is it?' She looked down at the box as though it were alive.

'Open it and see,' he said lightly, turning away from her and walking round to his place at the table opposite her, his big body easy and his face closed.

'Alex! I can't possibly accept this!' She stared down at the brilliant solitaire diamond surrounded by a little star of lacy gold fixed on a thin gold chain. It flashed its radiance from a bed of deep blue velvet and she almost stopped breathing as she thought of what the exquisitely wrought necklace must have cost. Why had he done this? The flower had been a piercingly sweet gesture, but this? This was a whole different ball-game.

'Don't you like it?' he asked mildly as he sipped a glass of wine slowly. 'You are at liberty to change it for something else if you like.'

'It's not that, you know it's not that,' she said quickly. 'No woman could fail to appreciate such a beautiful thing, but I can't possibly accept it. It must have cost a fortune.'

'The cost is incidental.' He leant forward suddenly, his eyes tight on her face. 'The flower reminded me of you and so did this, that's all there was to it. I saw them and liked them and it has given me pleasure to acquire them for you. Do you understand?'

'Alex...' She shook her head helplessly, her soft golden hair shining like silk. 'That's not the point. It's far, far too expensive. What would people think?'

'Does it matter?' The golden gaze narrowed. 'It's no one's business but our own. Do you really care what people think?'

She dropped her eyes before the directness, frightened her face would reveal her thoughts. She didn't care what misconstruction other people might put on the gift, it was true. That abrasive fire she had passed through all those years ago with Robin had cleansed her forever of needing people's approval. As long as she was right in her own heart nothing else had mattered since that purifying time. It wasn't the nameless crowd that worried her but him. She was worried what *he* would think if she accepted such a valuable present. Robin had tried to buy her in just the same way although she had been too naïve then to understand. She had no such excuse now. She couldn't accept the gift.

'I'm sorry, Alex.' She raised bruised blue eyes to meet his waiting face. 'It was very kind of you but I can't take this.' She snapped the lid shut and proffered the box to him. 'The flower is lovely—can we just leave it at that?'

He looked at her for a long moment, the rapier-sharp eyes boring into her mind as a coldness settled over the chiselled features, and then shook his head slowly. 'You think I'm trying to coax you into my bed with something like that?' His hand flicked scornfully at the box she still held. 'That I'm trying to tempt you into selling yourself? You do, don't you? Don't deny it.'

'I wouldn't deny it.' She held his glance bravely. 'It wouldn't be the first time someone in your position did something like that with a woman.'

'Well, it sure as hell would be the first time *I* did,' he snarled savagely, rising from the table violently and striding across to the huge full-length windows, pulling the heavy velvet curtains aside and standing with his back towards her, looking out into the snow-covered gardens beyond. She heard him swear softly to himself and then long minutes ticked by as he stood unmoving and she too remained like a statue, all thoughts numbed by the sudden storm. She heard him take a long deep breath as his shoulders straightened and then he turned to face her, his eyes hooded.

'That was the last thing on my mind, Fabia,' he said quietly. 'I know you well enough by now to understand that my wealth works against me, not for me, where you are concerned. I don't like the picture of me you have in your mind. I'm trying to understand, make allowances, but you sure don't make it easy. When I hold you in my arms your body tells me one thing but the rest of the time——' He stopped abruptly. 'What is it, Fabia? What makes you hate me?'

'I don't hate you, Alex,' she said painfully, the numbness melting in the face of his unexpected gentleness. 'I don't even know you——'

'Exactly.' He stared at her, his brow furrowed as his eyes bored into hers. 'And you don't intend to try to rectify that, do you.' It wasn't a question and she didn't try to answer it, her eyes falling down as her head lowered.

'Keep the pendant.' Her gaze raised to meet his. 'I would like to think of you wearing it some time, that's all. It's a Christmas gift, a thank-you for coming here with me if you like. You said you wouldn't accept any payment and I've taken a week of your time and placed you in difficult circumstances. Keep it.'

'Oh, Alex...' Her voice was soft but his face had set into harsh cold lines and he didn't look at her again as he resumed his place at the table, his movements abrupt.

She had hurt him, she realised in amazement. Offended him.

As Mary served the first course, her round plump face beaming and a sprig of holly fixed in the tight knot on the top of her head, Fabia sat in miserable silence, her head spinning. There was Susan, and maybe others like her, and yet he seemed so... sincere. But then maybe he was, she thought grimly, sincere in wanting a brief affair with her, sincere in telling her exactly where she stood from the word go, sincere in letting her see Susan. He hadn't tried to keep Susan from her and maybe he honestly believed he wasn't trying to buy her, but it all boiled down to the same thing in the end. As she spooned the delicious rich beef soup into her mouth her resolve strengthened. She couldn't be what he wanted her to be and if she tried the only person who would get hurt was her. She sensed instinctively that, if she had found the episode with Robin hard, *this* man could destroy her. She wasn't sure why—she kept the door to that avenue of thought firmly closed—but she knew it.

'A glass of wine?' She looked up to see Alex smiling coolly at her, his face bland, and like an actor taking a cue from a director she adopted the same pose as the meal progressed. She had five more days to get through and then she would be free and she would make sure she never, ever came into contact with Alexander Cade again.

'Mrs Cade has finished her meal, Mr Alexander.' Christine, Isabella's companion, stood in the doorway as they sipped their coffee. 'Are you coming to say goodnight?'

'Of course, Christine,' Alex said easily. 'Mary did us proud, didn't she? But it was a shame you and my grandmother couldn't join us.'

'Oh, we had our own little party upstairs, Mr Alexander,' Christine said comfortably. She paused and then moved closer to him, lowering her voice as she spoke again. 'I've suggested to Mrs Cade that she doesn't get up at all tomorrow. The company over the last two days has tired her more than she will admit.'

'I was thinking the same myself,' Alex agreed thoughtfully. 'She really seems very frail. Don't worry, Christine, I'll take care of it when I come up shortly.'

As the tall elderly woman left the room he turned to Fabia, his face polite but withdrawn. 'I shall be going to midnight mass in the village later. It's something that Isabella expects and it's little enough to do to please her. You are welcome to come along if you'd like to.' She hesitated, the instinctive refusal dying on her lips. She didn't want to be alone with him tonight with the atmosphere so tense and brittle, and yet... Neither did she want him to think she was nervous of him and the uncaring casualness of the invitation had made her feel contrary. He obviously didn't care one way or the other and she intended to let him see she felt exactly the same!

'I may as well,' she said lightly in the same tone he had used. 'I always find a Christmas Eve mass rather lovely.'

'Yes.' He smiled at her and there was something in the tawny-brown gaze that made her think, just for a minute, that in some way she had just played right into his hands. But that was nonsense and she was getting far too imaginative. She gave herself a mental shake.

'Just dress for warmth, a couple of jumpers and thick trousers,' he said nonchalantly. 'The dogs are in need of a walk and they'll wait outside while we're in the church so I thought it would be nice to go by foot rather than car. It isn't far, just a mile or so across the fields.'

'Fine,' she agreed quickly. If she was going to be alone with him it would be less dangerous to be in the great outdoors with the temperature well below freezing and two frisky dogs bounding by their side than in the warm intimacy of his car.

'You'll need a warm coat and boots,' he cautioned as he stood up to leave the room. 'The church is always only slightly warmer than the temperature outside and once one is sitting down the cold can really bite. I'll see you down here in an hour or so?'

She took him at his word and joined him in the hall some time later, buried under her big thick duffel coat, long scarf and mittens with her feet as warm as toast in sheepskin boots. He smiled slowly. 'You look like all the Christmas presents in the world rolled into one waiting to be unwrapped,' he said softly, touching the smooth softness of her cheek before donning his own thick car gloves. 'Come on, Major, Minor!' The two dogs bounded round their heels excitedly, tails wagging and shiny black noses ready for action.

As they stepped outside the shock of the icy frost-laden air made her gasp, but it was wonderfully exhilarating. The frost on top of the smooth white blanket of snow made the silver world surrounding them sparkle magically, the clear black sky overhead alive with a million twinkling stars.

'There's a short-cut through the grounds,' Alex said in her ear as he tucked her arm in his, 'then a mile over the fields and we're there. Are you game?'

She nodded, laughing suddenly as the two big dogs, wild with delight at the unexpected outing, rolled each other in the snow, barking madly in a confused welter of heads, paws and tails. 'Crazy pair of mixed-up kids,' Alex said indulgently. She glanced at his handsome face, alight with laughter and affection as he watched the antics of the dogs, and her heart lurched uncomfortably and then raced at twice its normal rate.

The night was clear and the moon was full, and as they walked through the fields arm in arm, following the path that other feet had trod that day but that was still inches thick in snow, she had a blinding sense of the significance of the moment. The starlit sky overhead, the rolling countryside clearly visible in its mantle of white, the exuberant animals and...Alex. She drank it all in without trying to understand why she felt so sweetly sad; now was not the time.

She felt dwarfed at his side in the flat-heeled boots but it was a good feeling. They didn't speak and curiously that was more intimate than any spoken words, and as the Christmas bells began to call the faithful to worship she knew a poignant shaft of pain in her heart that was more piercing than any of the agony she had endured with Robin.

'There's the church.' He looked down at her as he spoke, pointing across the white expanse in front of them to where a small stone-clad church complete with pencil-thin spire stood picturesquely under the dark sky. She had known it would look like that. The magic that had her in its grip had decreed it.

She couldn't remember the details of the service afterwards, just the heavy sweet smell of incense, the timeless beauty of the carols and the small crib at the front of the altar containing the Christ child. As they walked out into the cold crisp air to the waiting dogs she felt more miserable than she had ever felt in her life, and totally, helplessly confused.

'I'm glad you came.' He pressed her into his side as he spoke. 'Isabella was pleased when I told her.'

She looked up into his face slowly. And you, she wanted to ask; what, if anything, did it mean to you? The dogs walked quietly at their side now as if they too had been touched by the mystery of the night, and as they left the village lights and retraced their steps over the snow-lit fields he put an arm round her shoulders, drawing her close.

'It's Christmas Day,' he said softly as he brought her to a standstill, lifting her chin up to meet his gaze. 'Happy Christmas, angel-face.' His kiss was deep and fierce, his cold face touching hers as his lips plundered the sweetness of her mouth as though he was slaking a deep-rooted thirst.

She had known it would happen, planned that she would remain cool and unmoved, but the second she felt the pressure of his arms holding her close into the big body and his warm lips opening hers she was lost. The flame roared savagely, brightly, and when at last he lifted his mouth from hers they were both panting slightly, her eyes wide and dazed and his narrowed into bright gold slits.

'There's magic in the air, angel-face.' He slipped her arm through his and started walking, the dogs leaping up and padding by their side again, looking slightly puzzled at the strange behaviour of the humans who controlled their world.

'Magic?' Her voice was shaking slightly as she spoke and she hoped he wouldn't notice.

'Can't you feel it?' He looked down at her again, his face alive with emotion. 'The world decked out in bridal white as though it's waiting for us to——' He stopped abruptly and she licked suddenly dry lips, her heart thudding. For us to make love? she asked silently. It still comes down to that?

'Magic fades in the cold light of day,' she said quietly, 'and bridal white has a nasty habit of turning to black.'

'You don't believe that, not really.' He stopped again to look deeply into her face. 'You must believe in the power of love.'

'Why?' she asked coldly. 'It was love that put me on the steps of a hospital when I was a few hours old wrapped in an old newspaper. It was love that——' She stopped. She couldn't tell him about Robin; the humiliation had run too deep. 'I don't believe in love,' she finished expressionlessly.

'But you must want to get married one day, have children?' he persisted. 'Every girl wants a white wedding.'

'If I ever get married it will be in black as befits the occasion,' she said bitterly. 'Why pretend? Why play the game that everything is going to turn out all right in the end? It's fairy-tale nonsense.' She heard herself speaking the words with something akin to horror. Did she really believe that? she asked herself even as the words left her lips. She didn't want to feel like this, be this person she could hear talking so coldly, but it was the only way she could protect herself and stop the vulnerability from showing. Argue with me, Alex, she begged silently, convince me I'm wrong, give me some hope that I'm not going to spend the rest of my life alone.

He did none of those things as they continued their walk in silence, and as she glanced at his face from under her eyelashes she saw it was set in cold and austere lines now, the light that had been there a few minutes before just a memory.

As they reached the lights of the house he still didn't speak, not until they had divested themselves of their outer garments in the hall and she walked towards the stairs. 'You go up,' he said quietly as she turned to face him on the bottom step. 'I need a drink.'

He turned and walked into his empty sitting-room, the dogs following at his heels, as she walked slowly up the stairs and away from him, and suddenly that seemed forebodingly appropriate as the last drop of magic melted away.

CHAPTER EIGHT

IT WAS snowing again when Fabia awoke late Christmas morning after a restless, troubled night. Mary was pulling back the blinds, her good-natured face smiling as always, and Fabia saw a tray on the small table by her bed that the housekeeper must have brought in with her. 'Just a light snack of grapefruit and toast,' Mary said as she followed Fabia's gaze. 'Don't want to spoil your Christmas dinner and it's ten o'clock already.'

'Oh, I'm sorry, Mary,' Fabia apologised as she struggled into a sitting position in the soft bed. 'You shouldn't have bothered with a tray for me, you must have heaps to do.'

'No bother, Miss Fabia,' Mary replied warmly. 'I came in earlier but you looked so peaceful I didn't like to wake you.'

Peaceful? Fabia thought miserably. She hadn't known a moment's peace since she had met the master of this household, if the truth be known.

'Mr Alex has taken the dogs for a walk,' Mary continued cheerfully, 'but he'll be back in about half an hour and wondered if you'd like to come and see the mistress with him?'

'Yes, that'd be fine,' Fabia said quietly. 'I'll have breakfast and get dressed and come down, Mary. Is there anything I can do to help you this morning?'

'Help me?' Mary looked horrified. 'Oh, no, Miss Fabia, Cook and I have got everything under control. It wouldn't do for you to help.'

'No, I suppose not,' Fabia agreed slowly, 'but I'm not used to doing nothing. With looking after myself and the flat and doing a full-time job I usually haven't got a minute to spare.'

'Well, you just enjoy the luxury while it lasts, then,' Mary said brightly, 'but it was nice of you to ask, Miss Fabia, very nice.' She bustled off after placing the tray on Fabia's lap, her small body consumed with energy, and as Fabia ate she considered the small woman's words.

'Enjoy it while it lasts,' she repeated thoughtfully. The staff didn't expect her to be around again, then? The thought depressed her even though she had decided the same thing.

She was downstairs waiting for Alex when he returned from his walk, his face glowing and his bare head covered in snow. 'You should have worn a hat,' she admonished as he stood in the hall melting all over the thick carpet. 'You lose most of your body heat from the top of your head.'

'Really?' He cast a sardonic eye at her. 'And would you care if I was cold?' He was smiling as he spoke but she knew he meant the message the words were asking. 'Silly question, really,' he added as he gazed at her troubled face, 'and as I'm sure it's one you've got no intention of answering I won't wait for a reply.'

He glanced at the huge box she was holding in her arms. 'Isabella's present?' She nodded slowly. The tiny mirror was in her skirt pocket but she was wondering whether to give it to him or not now. 'Shall we go up, then?' He picked up several presents from under the tree in the main drawing-room first and then followed her up the stairs to his grandmother's room, where they spent a pleasant hour with the old lady, who was looking considerably better, but acceded grudgingly to Alex's repeated orders for her to stay in bed.

Fabia was touched to find that Isabella had bought her a gift, a superb dark leather handbag with a matching purse inside.

'You shouldn't have,' she said gratefully, her face expressing her pleasure more adequately than words, to which Isabella replied with a loud snort, although the old face was soft as it glanced at the young woman sitting on the bed.

Dinner was a traditional affair, a huge turkey with all the trimmings followed by plum pudding doused in brandy. It felt strange to be sitting with Alex at the beautifully decorated festive table in the lovely room surrounded by all the evidence of his wealth. She glanced at him as he spooned thick cream on to the rich pudding and her heart twisted painfully. At that moment she would have given the world for him to be a normal working man struggling to make ends meet—maybe then she would have had a chance? She caught at her thoughts abruptly. It was madness to think like this.

'I'm glad you're wearing it.' As the deep slumberous voice broke into her thoughts she raised her eyes to meet his. 'The pendant.' He touched his own neck. 'It suits you.'

'It's beautiful.' She forced a smile to her lips as she spoke and he nodded slowly, his eyes warm and soft with their strange glowing gold light.

'It has its own kind of loveliness but I prefer the flesh and blood kind... like yours.' He wasn't smiling as he spoke, and there was a strange kind of intimacy that had crept unbidden into the room. She stared at him dumbly. 'Thank you for coming here with me, Fabia,' he said softly as their eyes held and locked. 'It's been ...good.'

'Good?' She laughed sharply, purposely trying to break the mood before it took hold of her and her mind spiralled into the inevitable confusion he always managed to evoke. 'I got the impression I'm a trial and tribulation to you.'

'Did you?' He smiled slowly, his eyes dancing as he glanced at her defiant face. 'Well, maybe I'm due for a little trouble in my life right now.'

She didn't like him in this conciliatory mood, it was too…seductive. 'Yes…' For the life of her she couldn't think up a suitable crushing reply when faced with the questioning intensity that had now taken hold of his whole body. She sat, hardly daring to breathe, as he slowly rose from his chair, only to relax with an almost painful sense of anticlimax as the phone rang piercingly in the hall, shattering the mood into a hundred tiny pieces.

'Mr Alex?' Mary stood in the doorway as he resumed his seat, his face expressing his irritation. 'It's Miss Susan on the phone. She wonders what time the party begins tomorrow.'

'Susan?' He glared at poor Mary as though she were to blame for the spoilt moment. 'Same time as it does every year, I suppose,' he said abruptly. 'What's the matter with the woman?'

'I think she wants a word,' Mary said apologetically, and Alex snorted crossly.

'Tell her I'm eating,' he said coldly, ignoring his empty plate with regal indifference as Mary scuttled away.

'Party?' Fabia's heart had dropped like a stone.

'Oh, haven't I mentioned it?' he said with a little frown of annoyance. 'I meant to. It's one of Isabella's established laws that the whole of Cumbria congregates here on Boxing Day afternoon and unfortunately this year is no different.'

'Oh.' Fabia's voice was very small.

'We don't do much Christmas afternoon,' Alex said after the silence had stretched on and on interminably, 'but I hear one of the big lakes near by is frozen and being used for skating at the moment. We can either watch TV here or go there, whichever you'd prefer?' She caught his eyes fixed on her with a curious intensity as she glanced up but the next instant his expression had cleared into its usual remoteness.

'I'd love to go and watch at least,' she said eagerly, 'but I can't skate. I don't know how.'

'I'll teach you,' he said with a deep softness in his voice that brought a sudden hot flush to her face. 'We've several pairs of old skates somewhere; I'm sure we can find a pair to fit you.'

In ten minutes they were in the car with two pairs of skates on the back seat. It had stopped snowing but the sky was heavy and white and the air bitingly cold, all nature transfixed in its arctic grip. It was the start of a wonderful afternoon. When they arrived at the lakeside Fabia had the strangest impression that she had stepped back into Victorian times. The ice was alive with brightly coloured figures muffled to the eyebrows in long skirts and warm trousers and on the bank a man was selling hot roasted chestnuts, his glowing brazier vivid against the white snow.

The very air was intoxicating and Fabia made a sudden decision to take this afternoon, just this one, for herself, to enjoy this time with the tall handsome man at her side as though there had been no past and would be no future. Just the glorious present in all its poignant sweetness.

She discovered, to her delight, that she was a natural skater, and with Alex's arm about her waist and his hand holding hers in a firm supportive grip she found herself flying over the ice like a bird, gaining confidence every minute.

As the sky began to turn a soft rosy red they stopped for a cone of hot chestnuts, warming their hands in the heat of the brazier as they chatted to the other couples standing near by. She noticed that several of the women's eyes turned again and again to the tall and darkly vital man at her side but each time she glanced up into his face the golden-brown gaze was fixed on her, and when one of the women, more daring than the others, suggested they all swap partners for a time, he firmly declined, stating that as this was Fabia's first time on the ice he would trust her with no one but himself.

Even as the thrill of satisfaction shivered along her spine she found that other self cautioning her carefully, warning her silently that this was still Alexander Cade— just another facet that she hadn't seen before.

'I would have thought you would have liked to skate with that little redhead for a while,' she said lightly as they returned to the ice turned pink by the sky's fire overhead.

'Why?' he asked baldly, his eyes narrowed against the cold.

'Why?' The direct question floored her temporarily. 'Well...' She paused again. 'She's a very good skater,' she finished a little aggressively.

'Oh, I see,' he drawled softly, 'a very good skater? Maybe I prefer to stumble about with a very poor skater.' There was a coldness in the mocking taunt that warned her to leave the subject of the redhead alone, and after a few moments Alex began to show her how to spin and weave, laughing with her as in his efforts to save her from falling they both finished up in a heap on the ice.

'Nice state of affairs, this,' he grumbled laughingly as he helped her up from the ice, brushing the white flakes from her coat and adjusting her scarf more cosily round her face. She found little gestures like this almost unbearably painful, awakening as they did a whole host of abandoned dreams. There was something in his tenderness, his caring, that was more seductive than any lovemaking.

'You're a very complex man, aren't you, Alex?' she said softly, resisting his attempt to draw her back into the whirling arc of skaters. 'I wish I knew which was the real you.'

'The real me?' There was an expression of genuine bewilderment on his face. 'You've seen the real me, Fabia. What you see is what you get.'

'I don't believe that.' There was no amusement in her face now as she looked up into the dark golden gaze. 'I've heard you can be ruthless in business and I've seen you in action in the social scene, remember. All that doesn't tie up with...' She paused, uncertain of whether to continue.

'With the family man?' He had known how the sentence would finish. 'I thought you had more sense than that, Fabia. Of course I can't wear my heart on my sleeve when I'm conducting business negotiations; that side of my life is completely separate. As for my public face...that's what it is, a face. I put it on when necessary, it's as simple as that.'

'And the women?' She had to ask. 'Do you fool them the way you fool everyone else?'

'You're deliberately misunderstanding me.' He drew her away from the crowd and off the ice to a more secluded spot. 'If you are asking me if there have been women in my life then yes, Fabia, there have. *Have*, in the past. Each one meant something at the time although there was no great love story, I admit, but I have no intention of apologising to you or anyone else.' His eyes held hers intently. 'I'm a man, angel-face, an ordinary man with normal needs. I haven't lived like a monk but the things that are reported in the papers are absolute rubbish. If only a small fraction of them were true I'd probably be dead by now with physical exhaustion! I don't show everyone the real me, I grant you, but can you honestly say you do? That anyone does? There are very few people that one meets in a lifetime who really reach the core.'

'Oh, come on, Alex.' She took a step backwards as she spoke, away from his hand holding hers. The reference to the women he had known had hurt more than she would have thought possible in spite of her prompting it. 'On the one hand you are part of the jet-set and you said yourself you work hard and play hard——'

'There's nothing wrong with that,' he interrupted harshly, 'and I resent the term "jet-set". It implies something I am not. First and foremost I control my business empire, and that takes a great deal of time and effort. I have neither the time nor the inclination to waste my talents, and I do have a certain flair for the cut and thrust of my occupation, whether you believe it or not.' His face was cold and proud now and his big body stiff with pride. 'That is a separate part of my life, as I have said. It doesn't mean that ultimately I don't want what every man wants: a loving wife, happy home, children and so on.'

'You really believe that's what most men want?' she asked bitterly as a whole host of burning memories swept over her. 'Then your experience of the male sex must be very different from mine.'

'Unfortunately some men are arrogant and foolish,' he said slowly. 'They will discard a pearl along with the common stones in their avid search for the deception of experience. And some of the most heartless men I've known didn't have a penny to their names, incidentally.'

'We were talking about men, not money,' she said slowly, and he shook his head thoughtfully, his eyes glittering in the last rays of the dying sun.

'I have the feeling it's the same thing with you and that the two together add up to something...harmful?' She didn't answer the query in his voice and he stared at her for a full minute before turning away with a little gesture of disappointment. 'Still determined not to let me in, Fabia?' he asked grimly as he glanced at the darkening sky. 'The light's gone. We'd better get home.'

It was a cold, distant stranger who drove home, and as she glanced at his face once or twice under her lashes all the old doubts and suspicions came bubbling to the surface. He was still manipulating her, she thought wretchedly. He had admitted to it at the beginning of their relationship and nothing had changed, not really. He was rich and powerful and used to getting his own way, and unfortunately their circumstances, the season, the beauty all around them, everything was working to his advantage.

But she couldn't let her guard down. She had done it once all those years ago and nearly been destroyed in the process. She couldn't risk that again.

Mary served high tea in front of a huge roaring fire in the drawing-room later that evening and in spite of the mouth-watering sandwiches and light fluffy cakes Fabia found her appetite had deserted her completely. She had to stop this pointless longing for something that was as distant as the moon, it was tearing her apart, but the sight of him stretched out in the chair on the other side of the fire, his long legs toasting comfortably and his plate piled high with food, invoked a positively painful ache in her throat that made her eyes burn and her hands clench.

Mary came to collect the tea-trolley, cluck-clucking at the amount of food still left. 'Don't blame me, Mary,' Alex said teasingly, glancing at Fabia meaningfully.

'Aren't you hungry, Miss Fabia?' Mary asked quickly. 'You do look a bit peaky.'

'I'm fine, Mary, really.' Fabia smiled brightly. 'I made rather a pig of myself at lunchtime, I'm afraid.'

'Oh, as long as you're all right, then.' Mary bustled off as Alex lifted wry eyebrows.

'Another of your admirers, I'll be bound.' He joined her on the small two-seater sofa as he spoke, placing a casual arm round her shoulders as he sat down. 'Still, I suppose it's no surprise that she likes you; they all do.' She had stiffened at his approach and now turned to him, her face cold.

'There have been people who didn't,' she said coolly as she moved a fraction of an inch away from him, 'and please take your arm away, Alex. We're alone now, there's no need to act.'

'Is that what I'm doing?' A certain inflexion in his voice had changed now, its tone deeper and with a trace of iron in its depths. 'I can't put a friendly arm around you now?'

'No.' And you're not going to put me in the wrong again, she thought silently as she stared coldly into the handsome face inches away from her own.

'Why so hostile, Fabia?' His body hadn't moved an inch but in some subtle way it seemed more menacing now than affectionate. 'I'm getting a little tired of the constant assumption that I'm only capable of having one thing on my mind.'

'I'm not assuming anything,' she said quickly, 'but as far as I'm concerned *you* made the suggestion that you employ me for a specific task and nothing else. Not a foot or a toe out of place, I think you said? Well, that works both ways.'

'Does it, indeed?' He turned in the seat to stare straight into her face, his eyes slanted dangerously. 'What a bossy little female you are, my pet.' As he leaned towards her he moved his arms and body in such a way that she found herself pinned against the sofa so that she couldn't move, his hard rigid body trapping her as his face moved down towards hers.

She had expected a hard fierce kiss to follow through on the act of dominance, but instead she found his lips brushing down on hers, tracing the outline of her face with light feathery kisses in between parting her lips tantalisingly and circling her ears with his hot clean breath. It was impossible to stop the flood of desire that began to rise as he continued the sensual teasing game. She could feel every inch of his steel-hard frame against her melting softness and tried desperately to hide the quivering response the practised seduction was bringing forth, hating herself for her weakness at the same time as she wanted to moan her pleasure against his hard face.

The probing tongue reached deeper now with each return to her mouth, tasting the sweetness within greedily before leaving to burn a fiery trail over her upturned face and throat, his hands moving over her body with sure knowledge of how to please as he brought forth little whimpers of exquisite pain. She had never felt like this in her life, as though a blazing inferno was eating her up, but even as the storm of passion carried her along she knew it was a calculated exercise on his part, and despair at her vulnerability gnawed at her pride.

'There, now.' As he raised his head she lay for a moment stunned in his arms before opening dazed blue eyes as he rose slowly to his feet. 'Before you give out your orders to me again just think long and hard, would you, about who wants what?' The honey-brown eyes raked her flushed face mockingly as he walked towards the door. 'I'm not some sort of animal waiting to leap on you and have my wicked way, angel-face. If I had wanted you it wouldn't have been rape, would it?' He turned at the door and surveyed her once again as she sat up hastily, smoothing her hair with shaking, numb fingers. 'I happen to feel it would be necessary for you to want me as much as I want you before anything would happen, and I don't mean just in the physical sense.' The eyes were razor-sharp now. 'When you come to me it will be because you want to, heart, mind *and* body.'

'Never.' The whisper was faint, but he heard it, and the handsome face hardened.

'Never is a long time, little girl.'

As the door closed behind him Fabia sat in front of the hot, leaping flames, feeling icy cold right through, her thoughts spinning in a whirling circle of confusion. She had known he could be ruthless but the cold-blooded determination he had displayed in setting out to prove to her that she was defenceless against him had unnerved her more than she had thought possible.

'I don't understand you, Alexander Cade,' she murmured into the empty room after long, slow minutes had ticked by in the stillness broken only by the crackle of the burning coal. She wanted to think he had been trying to humiliate her, crush her; that would fall into line with what she thought of him, and yet...

Her mind ground to a halt. He could have had her tonight, they both knew that, and he hadn't. It hadn't been because he didn't want to either; the hard firm body pressed so close to hers had revealed his thrusting desire too clearly for that. Did she believe him when he said that he wanted her to want him in the way he had described, and, if so, why? Why not be content with her body and leave it at that? She brushed her hand across her eyes and saw it was wet with tears, and yet she hadn't been aware she was weeping. She didn't understand him!

Much later, as she lay in the warm softness of her bed, her eyes seeking the darkness for an answer to her despair, bitter memories of Robin's cruelty crept unbidden into the confusion. She had trusted him implicitly, and was he really any different from Alex in what he wanted? Alex had already said that the main reason for her being here was because he wanted no entanglements, no romantic involvement to complicate his busy life once the Christmas season was over. Why was she even considering trusting him? Once she had served her purpose he would return to Susan and her kind without a backward glance.

Susan... She pictured the brunette's long, glossy dark hair and deep green eyes with their thick black lashes and shivered despite the warmth of the covers. And there were the children too. Alex clearly adored them and Susan knew it.

She turned over in the bed, bringing the pillow down on her head as though it could shut out the thoughts that were tormenting her. It was hopeless, absolutely hopeless.

She rose early the next morning before the rest of the household was awake, taking a long leisurely shower before washing her hair and drying it slowly, brushing its sleek richness into shining golden waves. Somehow she needed to look her best the next time she saw him. She applied light, careful make-up before donning tight, figure-hugging trousers in a soft cream wool and a big baggy fluffy jumper of the same shade. It was a casual outfit but one she knew complemented her colouring perfectly, and she needed all the help she could get today. Later, at the party... She forced her mind away from Susan with dogged determination.

Alex appeared briefly at breakfast, his face tight and restrained, and then closed himself in his study with terse instructions that he wasn't to be disturbed. 'Is everything all right, Miss Fabia?' Mary asked anxiously as she bustled in with fresh coffee mid-morning as Fabia sat idly looking through a stack of magazines in the main drawing-room.

'I suppose so, Mary,' Fabia said as lightly as she could, 'but to be honest I'm bored out of my mind without something to do. Alex is busy and Isabella is still sleeping and I'm just not used to doing nothing.' She smiled wryly at the little housekeeper. 'I'd never make one of the idle rich, would I?'

'I don't know about that, Miss Fabia, but you could do the flowers for the party tonight if you really do want something to do. Jenny is rushed off her feet with the amount of cooking there's still to do and I'm tied up with a million and one last-minute details. It'd really be a help if you wouldn't mind.'

'Would it?' Fabia smiled delightedly. 'I'd love to. Lead me to them.' Anything to keep her mind from the destructive circle it seemed intent on following, she thought gratefully.

By mid-afternoon all the preparations were complete and with Isabella installed in the drawing-room ready to greet the first guests Fabia hurried upstairs to change. She hadn't seen Alex since morning. He had ordered sandwiches and coffee in the study at lunchtime and she understood he had paid a brief visit to his grandmother's room before lunch, but apart from that he was incommunicado.

It was as she was finishing putting the last touches to her make-up that the light knock sounded at the door, and, thinking it was Mary or Christine with a message from Isabella, she called a cheerful 'come in' as she turned round on the tiny dressing-table stool.

'I wanted a word with you before we go downstairs.' Alex stood in the doorway, devastatingly handsome in an off-white lounge suit with pale blue shirt and tie, his long hair slicked back and his golden-brown eyes glinting strangely.

'Oh...' She stared at him mesmerised as he walked towards her, stopping a foot or so away and leaning against the wall as he took in her slender shape in the dark wine cocktail dress she had decided to wear for the evening's gaiety. She had twisted her hair into a casual knot on the top of her head, leaving several silky floating strands of hair wisping about her neck, the diamond pendant lying in the hollow of her throat like a piercingly beautiful teardrop.

'I think an apology is in order.' For a crazy moment she thought he was asking that she apologise to him, and then he cleared his throat slowly and spoke again. 'I'm sorry for acting in such a ... cavalier way last night, Fabia. It was unforgivable and it won't happen again. I thought when I brought you here that you would understand——' He stopped abruptly. 'That you would see——' He stopped again and swore softly. 'Suffice it to say I won't be troubling you with my unwelcome intentions again. OK?'

It wasn't, but she couldn't explain to him what she didn't understand herself, and she merely nodded slowly as he inclined his head towards her and strode from the room, shutting the door firmly behind him. She took a long deep breath before turning slowly on the delicate little stool and looking at her reflection in the long, ornate mirror. That was that, then. She had sensed that he had reached some sort of decision. Maybe he would ask her to leave early tomorrow, but then how could he explain such action to Isabella? She shut her eyes for a moment and swayed back and forwards with her arms tight around her waist as a shaft of pure agony pierced her heart. She didn't want to leave him. The thought shocked her with its fierceness and she opened bruised blue eyes to stare reproachfully at the pale, slim girl in the mirror. 'Don't be so pathetic,' she said softly. 'You go down there now and you act like you've never acted before. None of this is real, it never was.'

As the guests began to arrive she was aware, as she stood by Isabella's side, that she was waiting for just one beautiful face in the throng that was slowly filling the huge house. She saw the children before she saw Susan, Gemma looking like a little angel in a frothy party dress of white velvet and Jeremy trying to act the man in a small cream suit with a little red dicky-bow. They looked delightful...and they were, she thought miserably. How someone like Susan came to have such warm, natural children she would never know. The answer to that was revealed later as she watched Susan's parents attend to their grandchildren's needs while Susan floated about in an elegant swirl of dark green silk, looking as though she had spent all day getting ready—which she probably had, Fabia thought tightly.

'Their father adored them,' Isabella said softly in her ear at one point early into the party as she watched the children standing dutifully by the side of their grand-parents, their small hands clasped in those of the grown-ups. 'They were the only bright spots in the poor man's life once he'd taken Susan on,' she carried on quietly. 'She made poor William's life hell.'

'Did she?' Fabia looked sharply at the old lady, who smiled at her understandingly.

'Anything in trousers, my dear,' Isabella said blithely, unaware of how incongruous the term sounded on her lips. 'Poor William was sent to an early grave.'

'*She* called him "poor William",' Fabia said thought-fully, making up her mind in that instant that she was going to stand no nonsense from Susan tonight. Or any other time, if it came to it!

'Crocodile tears, my dear,' the old lady said firmly. 'The girl's bad all through.' Fabia glanced at the tiny figure affectionately. Like a true Italian Isabella loved and hated with equal passion; there was nothing lukewarm about her emotions even at her great age.

Within minutes Alex appeared at her side and re-mained close by for the next hour or two although Fabia got the distinct impression that it was more to further Isabella's pipe-dreams than any wish to be near to her.

'Wake up, young lady! You've got some explaining to do.'

'What . . . ?' She jolted upright, her heart pounding, coming to as she took in her surroundings and saw Alex bent over her, his dark face breathing fire. 'What on earth do you want and what time is it?'

'What time is it?' He repeated her words in cold mockery as he stood upright, his eyes searing over her creamy full breasts, revealed clearly through the whisper-thin nightie she was wearing. 'If you had been where you should be, next to me in full view of all my guests, you would know what damn time it was! Why did you disappear like that?'

'Why did I . . . ?' She spluttered out of words as sheer unadulterated rage took her over, her anger making her quite unaware of the seductive figure she made as she sat amid the tumbled covers with her hair streaming across her shoulders and her violet eyes huge in her flushed face. 'You dare to ask me that!' She knelt up in her rage, her hand going out to strike the handsome face above her, but he caught her wrist in an iron grip as his eyes narrowed.

'No, you don't, angel-face.' His grip tightened as she struggled until she gasped with pain. 'And I repeat my question. Why did you leave the party like that without even telling me you were going? If nothing else it was the height of rudeness.'

She stared at him angrily without speaking. If he thought she was going to object verbally to him making a fool of himself with Susan he had another think coming. He could do what he liked with whom he liked but she was blowed if she was going to sit and watch like some pathetic little bimbo grateful for crumbs from the great man's table.

'Well?' As his gaze lowered to her body she suddenly became aware of just how little she had on at the same time as she realised his breathing had thickened. 'Are you going to answer me?'

She pulled the duvet up round her breasts with her free hand, glaring at him ferociously. 'You're the one who controls an empire,' she spat furiously. 'You figure it out.'

He held her glance tightly, speaking quietly now through clenched teeth. 'You drive me to the limit, woman,' he said thickly. 'Right at this moment I want to take you until you're crying out for more, until the things I do to you drive you crazy with desire and there is no one in your world except me.'

'I'd hate you,' she said bitterly, trying to wrestle her wrist free, and then froze as he laughed softly, his eyes glittering in the dim light.

'You do anyway.' His gaze lowered again to her body, the duvet having slipped in her frantic struggles, and suddenly his arm swept round her waist as he pulled her close, his body falling against her on the softness of the bed.

She wanted to fight him and in those first few seconds she did, silently and with all her might, and then she became aware of the hard muscular thighs pressed close to hers and the trembling that caught hold of her limbs drove all the strength from her body.

He hadn't kissed her until that point but now his lips fastened on hers and she felt as though every nerve-ending in her body had been sensitised into one glorious whole. As his hands stroked down her body, ruthlessly determined at first and then, as he sensed her compliance, dizzyingly, erotically soothing, she knew she was lost. She was enthralled by the sensations he invoked so easily, entranced by the sheer heady excitement that he wanted her, wanted her so badly that he was groaning her name against her hot flesh. She hadn't expected it to feel so right.

She knew, as his body shuddered against her, that he was holding himself in an iron restraint as he coaxed her desire still further, and the more she responded, the more she gave of herself, the more unhurried and restrained he seemed to be, kissing her face, her throat, her breasts with soft, sensual, undemanding kisses that, even as they reassured, fired her to strain against him in an agony of need.

'Do you understand now, Fabia?' he whispered softly as he stroked her with long, sensitive movements that caused an exquisite pleasure to pulse in time with her heartbeat. 'It could be so good, I can make you want me as much as I want you. All you have to do is let me...' She could barely hear him, her senses disorientated and lost in an explosion of feeling, and as she sighed mindlessly his voice became more insistent.

'Fabia? Listen to me. You have to want this in your mind as much as your body; I'm not settling for second-best. Do you hear me?'

'Second-best...?' As she pulled herself back into the cold light of reason it was to see his face, inches from her own, his dark gold eyes blazing with passion and... something else, something she couldn't understand.

'I'm me, Alexander Cade, I won't be a substitute for anyone else, in bed or out of it.' They were still entwined in each other's arms and for a fleeting moment she wished he hadn't spoken, wished his hands and mouth had continued to do their devastating work which would have ended in only one conclusion. And then she realised where she was, who she was and the fact that she was stark naked in his arms, her nightie having obviously been discarded some time along the way without her even being aware of it.

'Do you care for me, even a little?' As she tried to jerk herself out of his embrace he held her still tighter. 'Do you?'

'Let go of me.' How could he ask her that? What sort of woman did he think she was? That she invited this from anyone? Of course she cared for him; she—— The door in her mind slammed shut. He had got under her skin, that was all. That had to be all. 'Please, Alex, let me go.'

He held her for one long moment more and then slid his feet over the side of the bed flinging the duvet over her nakedness as he did so, his face set in a mask of tight control although she noticed, with a small dart of surprise, that his hands were shaking as he stood up and moved across to the dressing-table, resting both hands on the smooth marble surface as he bent down with head lowered and legs apart. 'That's that, then.' His voice was husky and deep. 'Now I know where I stand.' She couldn't reply, she was beyond speech, her mind spiralling in such a whirlwind of confusion that it was a physical pain.

As he kept his head lowered she saw his hand move out to touch something on the dressing-table top and realised with a little dart of horror that she had left his present there the day before, unable to make up her mind whether to give it to him or not, unsure of how he would react.

He picked it up, reading the little card as he did so, and then turned to look at her, his eyes remote and un-fathomable. 'Do I take it this was meant for me, or is the Alex on the top of the card someone else?'

'Of course it was meant for you,' she said shakily. 'I just changed my mind, that's all.'

'A woman's prerogative.' His eyes returned to the tiny package in his hands. 'May I?' She nodded helplessly, her face white.

As he opened the small box and held the tiny key-ring aloft the little mirror flashed in a ray of moonlight from the window and he remained perfectly still for a moment. 'Thank you.' He slipped the box into his pocket. 'I shall treasure this, whatever the motive was in buying it.'

She stared at him, mesmerised by the compelling look on his face, a composite of pain, hunger, anger and ... something else she couldn't place. He turned and walked to the door, twisting on the threshold to glance across at her again, the strangeness still visible in his tight jaw and shadowed eyes. 'And I do know, Fabia,' he said quietly, his voice now devoid of all emotion.

'You know?' she whispered in bewilderment.

'Who caught who.' A tiny muscle flickered for a moment in the hard jaw. 'But how was I to know how much it would hurt?'

As the door slammed behind him she shuddered for a second at the constrained savagery with which he had closed it, and then buried her head deep in the soft pillow as hot tears flooded her eyes.

'But how was I to know how much it would hurt?' What did that mean—after an evening spent with Susan? This whole thing was a maze, a minefield of half-spoken suggestions and confusing innuendoes, and if she took the wrong path ... She shook her head as the wet pillow stuck to her cheeks. Alex, oh, Alex ... There had been something in his face as he had left that had frightened her, a tight coldness, as though he had reached a decision that was painful but irrevocable. She fell asleep as dawn touched the night sky with tentative fingers, confused, frightened and desperately alone.

CHAPTER NINE

THE next three days passed as if in a dream. The arctic weather still held the world outside in a breathtakingly beautiful icy grip but Alex didn't suggest they visit the lake again. They went on a couple of long walks with the dogs and visited some old friends of Isabella's, but Alex had departed from her in some unfathomable way, although he was as attentive and polite to her in private as when they were in company. He made no effort to touch her now when they were alone and even his endearments for Isabella's benefit were restrained. If his grandmother noticed that something was amiss she didn't mention it, although Fabia caught the bright robin eyes glancing at them more than once.

When she awoke on the morning of her departure she lay for some time in the big warm bed, gazing out of the window at the white lacy pattern Jack Frost had painted on the glass, unable to believe that she was going to say goodbye to Isabella and the rest of the household that day. Now the time was here she felt suddenly bereft and utterly alone, her stomach clenched in a giant knot and a feeling of something like panic sending fluttering shivers down her limbs. She wouldn't allow herself to think of Alex, not for a minute, a second.

She had packed the night before and now, after a quick shower, she dressed slowly in trousers and a warm jumper, looping her hair into a high ponytail and wearing no make-up except for a light touch of blue on her eyelids.

As she entered the big breakfast-room Alex looked up from behind his paper and just for a moment, before the heavy veil dropped down over his eyes, she thought she saw a flash of something almost like pain in the tawny gaze. 'Good morning, Fabia.' As the deep rich voice spoke her name it registered on her for the first time that there had been no 'angel-face' since the day of the party, and again she felt a loss she had no right to feel. 'Your day of release.' He smiled grimly. 'All good things come to those who wait.'

He wasn't joking and she didn't smile, merely inclining her head towards him before going to the long sideboard and helping herself from the covered dishes of scrambled egg, mushrooms, tomatoes and fried ham and sausages. 'What time do you want to leave?' she asked quietly as she seated herself at the table.

'After lunch.' His voice was abrupt. 'The roads aren't too bad now we haven't had any fresh falls of snow for a few days so we should be able to drive straight back without too much difficulty.'

She nodded slowly. He obviously wanted to get rid of her as quickly as possible now her mission was accomplished. The shaft of pain she felt almost took her breath away but as she continued eating, mechanically, the little voice of logic reassured her that it was probably the best thing. She had no place in his world so the sooner she left it the better.

'Miss Fabia?' Christine's grey head peered round the breakfast-room door. 'Mrs Cade would like a word with you later if that's all right. She's feeling tired so she isn't getting up today. Perhaps you'd take mid-morning coffee with her about eleven?'

'Of course.' Fabia looked at the elderly companion in concern. 'Is she well, Christine? I mean, she's not——?'

'I think all the excitement of the last few days has worn her out,' Alex said quietly. 'She would insist on having a grand sort of Christmas despite all advice to the contrary, almost as if she senses . . .' His voice trailed away and he rose from the table stony faced. 'She's just tired, Fabia, that's all. She is eighty-seven, after all.'

She wanted to offer some word of comfort to him as he strode from the room but there was nothing she could say. His grandmother *was* an old, old lady with a weak heart and she knew her imminent death would hit him hard. She had been mother and father to him all his life, after all. Maybe it was his anxiety for Isabella that had turned him into this cold, reserved stranger with his carefully polite voice and distant smiles? Or maybe he's just fed up with me, she thought miserably. Their relationship had hardly been a smooth one, after all.

The big grandfather clock in the hall was chiming eleven as she knocked on Isabella's door later that morning. As before, the tiny woman seemed lost in the huge bed, but Fabia was relieved to see that she was as bright-eyed as usual, with vocal cords intact.

'Come and sit by me, child, don't dither!' Fabia joined her by the bed with a wry smile twisting her lips. It would take more than exhaustion to quell Isabella's sharp tongue. 'Now, you're leaving after lunch, so Alexander tells me?' Fabia nodded slowly.

'I'd like to thank you for such a lovely holiday,' she began politely, but Isabella's lined face pulled itself into an irritated grimace and she waved a hand in front of Fabia's face, bidding her silence.

'Be quiet, girl. I want to have a little talk with you and we haven't got much time. I can never be alone in this house for long, always someone coming to bother me.' She glanced up at Fabia, her black eyes piercing under the shock of snow-white hair. 'Now, then, I like you, Fabia Grant, I like you very much.'

'Thank you.' Fabia stared at her in surprise.

'And because I like you I am going to say things which you may think impertinent, but then I'm an old lady, so...' She shrugged graphically with the twist of her shoulders that was pure Latin.

'I don't usually care for the women my grandson attracts,' she said blandly as Fabia stared at her wide-eyed. 'There have been one or two who have been...acceptable, but not what I would choose for him, not at all.' Fabia flushed scarlet, her cheeks burning hot. 'You, as I say, are different and he knows it. I brought him up to recognise the wheat from the chaff and I wouldn't like to see him hurt.'

'I don't understand.' Fabia stared into the lined old face in confusion.

'I'm not saying he hasn't sown some wild oats, mind, but then you'd hardly expect him to have reached the age of thirty-five without having had a few...encounters, would you?' Fabia shook her head dazedly. 'But he knows a diamond when he sees one.' The black eyes held hers fast. 'You understand me, child?'

'Look, Isabella...' Fabia paused, uncertain of how to continue. The whole point of her being here had been to give Isabella's last days the comfort of thinking that her grandson just might have met the right girl at last, but it was all supposed to have been vague hopes and dreams. This direct confrontation was not at all what she had supposed but then, knowing Isabella as she now did, she *should* have known, she thought wryly!

'You know he cares for you, girl? That he cares very deeply indeed?' Now Fabia rose from the chair at the side of the bed with a little gesture of repudiation that was instinctive rather than tactful in the circumstances.

'I'm sorry, Isabella, I don't think things are quite what you think, not yet at any rate,' she added hastily. 'Alex——'

'Alex is in love with you, my dear,' the old lady said flatly.

'Has he told you that?' Fabia forgot to pretend as she met the old lady's tight gaze.

'No, not in so many words,' Isabella admitted slowly. 'But I've seen the way he looks at you, child. He's never looked at another woman like that and besides,' she paused reflectively, 'it's just the way my dear husband used to look at me.'

'It is?' Fabia realised her mouth was wide open and shut it with a little snap. 'But I don't think——'

'This is a cosy little huddle.' The deep voice from the doorway interrupted them seconds after a brief cursory knock. 'Is it private or can anyone join in?'

'See what I mean?' Isabella said to Fabia with a resigned little shrug. 'Never a minute to myself, visitors, visitors all day long. And then they wonder why I'm tired . . . ?' She looked up at her grandson as he crossed the room to stand by her side, the wealth of love in her eyes belying the harshness of her words. 'You can both kiss me goodbye now,' she added grandly. 'I shall sleep directly afer lunch.'

They left the room a few minutes later with Isabella's words ringing in Fabia's ears, and as she ate the light lunch Mary had prepared for them in the comfort of Alex's sitting-room she glanced at his sombre, distant face once or twice, seeking something, anything, that would indicate Isabella was right. But there was nothing in the cold, slightly cruel slanted eyes that gave her any hope and his face could have been cut in stone, such was the lack of expression on the chiselled features.

They left the house just after one, with Mary's goodbyes ringing in her ears and the dogs' mournful eyes when they spotted the suitcases making her more depressed than ever.

'Isabella asked me to tell you that she would like you to visit again soon,' Alex said suddenly after they had driven a few miles in complete silence. 'Do you think that may be possible?' There was a certain inflexion in his voice, a tilt to his head, that made a surge of wild hope flare briefly, only to die as quickly as cold reason inserted itself grimly into her head.

He wanted what he considered was the best for his grandmother at the moment, she told herself flatly, and he had warned her at the outset of all this that Isabella was a born matchmaker. 'Maybe,' she said quietly. 'Let's just play it by ear, shall we?'

He turned quickly to give her a flash of a smile that had some of the old warmth in it, and as he did so her heart turned over. 'Suits me,' he said lightly. 'I'll be in touch.' That wasn't quite what she had meant but somehow the feeling that had swamped her so fiercely had taken her breath away and she let his remark go unanswered, more shaken than she cared to admit. It's just physical attraction, she told herself as the powerful car ate up the miles effortlessly, that's all. He's stirred your senses, but so what? It doesn't mean anything.

By the time they reached the grey streets of London, filled with black watery slush and tall austere buildings grimy and grim in the dim half-light, the light, crisp white world she had left behind seemed a million miles away. This is reality, she told herself silently as Alex drove towards her flat; come down to earth, girl, before he breaks you into a hundred little pieces.

'You're a wonderful advertisement for the beauties of Cumbria,' Alex said drily as they drew up outside her block of flats which looked even grubbier than normal. 'Could you just try and pretend that you've enjoyed yourself, if only to ease my guilt?' There was a dark mockery in the words that hurt her but she forced her voice to be as light as his as she replied.

'I've had a lovely time, thank you, Alex, and I'm sure the guilt is only a momentary lapse. There's no need to come up,' she added hastily as he reached for her suitcase on the back seat, 'it's not heavy.'

'Don't be silly,' he said mildly as he helped her out of the car and followed her into the building after locking the car doors. 'Isabella would never forgive me if you were accosted on the last lap.' She smiled tightly. Damn Isabella, she thought suddenly, and you and the whole caboodle!

As she opened the door and switched on the light the little flat reached out to her welcomingly, and foolishly she had to bite back the tears before turning to Alex, her hand held out in farewell. 'Goodbye, Alex, and thank you again.'

He raised an eyebrow at the outstretched hand but took it anyway, raising it to his mouth before turning it over and gently kissing the palm in a long lingering caress. She had the urge to snatch it away but controlled it masterfully, keeping a bland smile on her face as he raised his head and looked straight into her face. 'I'll phone you,' he said huskily, his eyes bright in the artificial light.

She shrugged carefully. 'If you get time,' she said coolly as he let go of her hand that was burning where his lips had touched. 'I know you're a very busy man.'

He gave her one last long unsmiling look and then stepped backwards out of the door, closing it behind him as he went, and she was alone.

The next few days limped by in a confusion of disorientated thinking, sudden flashes of sharp knife-like pain and nights of crying. She made more mistakes at work in seven days than she had in the whole of the seven years she had worked there, couldn't eat, couldn't sleep and began to feel she was going slowly crazy...and still Alex didn't call.

As she left work on the Friday night, ten days after Alex had brought her home and disappeared out of her life, she found she was dreading the weekend ahead.

All this has just brought back all the old memories about Robin, she told herself for the hundredth time as she made her way through the busy London streets crowded with dour-faced commuters; it's no more than that. Give it a few more days and you'll be back to your old self. He's just unsettled you, that's all. Was he seeing Susan again? He could be with her now, this second—how would she ever know? He had obviously decided not to contact her again, anyway—that much at least was clear.

As a solitary snowflake landed on her nose she glanced up into the heavy white sky angrily. And now it was going to snow again! Even the elements seemed intent on reminding her of him at every turn. Well, she'd had enough of this! She *was* going to stop feeling sorry for herself, she *was* going to get back to being the old Fabia who was in control of her life and her destiny, and no six-foot-four Adonis with dark hair and tawny eyes was going to stop her.

As she turned the corner and saw the big sedate Bentley parked outside the flats her stomach jumped into her mouth and she came to an abrupt stop, causing several people behind her to cannon into each other like a human train. She didn't even hear the irate man behind her growling an insult about women pedestrians; all her energies were concentrated on the big tall figure uncurling himself from the car interior, his honey-flecked eyes tight on her face across the distance separating them. Calm, now, calm, she warned herself silently as she walked towards him on legs that were suddenly wobbly.

'Fabia.' Her name was a caress in itself as the low rich voice reached out to her and as he reached her side he bent and deposited a swift kiss on her wet hair. The sky was full of whirling flakes of snow now and already the ground was turning a virginal white. 'How are you?'

'I'm fine, thank you,' she said quietly as she inwardly mocked herself for the inanity of her reply. I'm terrible, Alex, she told him silently, and I don't know why. I'm falling apart, can't you see?

'I've been abroad,' he said slowly. 'America. Only got back today.' He stared at her silently.

'I see.' She nodded quietly. Say something, Alex, she said silently. Tell me you're pleased to see me, that you wanted to come, anything!

'I'm here to ask you a favour, again,' he said softly, and she noticed that there were tight lines of strain round his mouth and a weary hunch to his broad shoulders under the black coat. 'It's Isabella.'

For a brief piercingly painful moment she acknowledged that he hadn't come to see her because he had wanted to but because he needed something from her, and then that realisation was pushed aside as anxiety for the old lady who had been so kind to her asserted itself. 'What's wrong?' She stared at him wide-eyed. 'She's not——?'

'She's taken a turn for the worse.' He brushed his hair back from his forehead and she noticed there was a grey tint of exhaustion to the handsome face. 'John called me back from America because he was concerned about her and by the time I arrived she wasn't too good.' He flexed his shoulders tiredly. 'I had a few minutes with her but she's got it in her head that she wants to see you and nothing I said could dissuade her.' You wanted to dissuade her, she asked him silently, you didn't want to see me?

'Would you mind coming with me again, Fabia?' he asked softly. 'I know it's a lot to ask, feeling about me the way you do.'

'Feeling about you...?' she asked bewilderedly.

'I know I'm probably the last person in the world you want to see right now, but it's important to her,' he continued slowly. 'Could you put your dislike of me aside for a day or two? Please?' His voice was infinitely weary.

'Of course I'll come with you, Alex,' she said quietly. 'Come inside and I'll pack a bag.' As she hurriedly filled her small overnight case she purposely kept her mind blank, numbing her emotions in case they let her down. He looks ill, she thought as she left her bedroom to find him waiting by the open front door, leaning against the wall, eyes shut.

'Why didn't you sit down?' She indicated an easy-chair in the lounge, her eyes wide with concern.

'If I sit down I'm worried I shan't get up again,' he said with a poor attempt at a smile. 'I haven't slept in the last thirty-six hours and I wasn't sleeping too well before then. Don't worry, Swinton's driving.'

'I wasn't thinking about who was driving,' she said sharply, and he winced slightly at her tone.

'Not tonight, Fabia,' he said softly. 'I really do believe I'm at the end of my tether, so just be a good girl and come quietly.' He smiled again but it didn't reach the glazed gold of his eyes. 'Are you ready?'

Once in the warm interior of the big car he stretched out his legs with a weary groan, taking her hand in his as she sat beside him. 'You don't mind, do you?' he asked with a nod at his hand holding hers. 'I just need to hang on to something at the moment.'

'Glad to oblige,' she said lightly past the lump in her throat. He looked suddenly vulnerable, younger, quite different from the hard, ruthless image of him she had carefully built up in her mind over the last ten days.

'That's all right, then.' Even as he murmured the words he was asleep, and as the weather worsened into the blizzard conditions they had endured on the first journey she was immensely grateful for the big powerful car and the solid Swinton sitting silently behind the wheel. More than once her heart was in her mouth during the long drive and although the backs of her eyes ached with tiredness she couldn't relax, vitally conscious of the dangerous conditions and even more of the exhausted man at her side, his dark head resting on her shoulder. She tried to quell the tenderness that was uppermost as she glanced down at him now and again but it was a tide that was unstoppable, and by the time the car drove into the long winding drive her emotions were raw.

'Alex.' She shook him gently and he opened dazed eyes that widened on seeing her face so close to his.

'Fabia.' He had taken her mouth in a long slow kiss before she realised what was happening and for a moment time was suspended as they clung together in the quietness of the car. Then Swinton coughed loudly as he climbed out of the driver's seat and opened the door on Alex's side.

'We've arrived, Mr Cade.' Alex came to with almost a start of surprise and stared vacantly for one more moment before realisation dawned.

'Of course.' Suddenly he was the efficient executive again, out of the car and round to her side before she could move and taking her arm as they walked through the thick snow to the front door. 'I must have slept the journey away,' he said in tones of comical amazement. 'I'm sorry, Fabia, very rude of me.'

'Don't be silly,' she said lightly. 'You were absolutely tired out.' The feel of his mouth on hers was still with her as they entered the house, and its warmth stayed with her until they entered Isabella's room and she saw just how ill the old lady was. The mauve lips tried to say her name as she leant over the bed but there was just the faintest whisper on the air and even that slight effort seemed to tire the tiny figure.

'Don't try and talk, Isabella,' Fabia said gently. 'I just wanted you to know I'm here with Alex and we're staying with you until you're better.' She saw a glimmer of understanding in the tired eyes fixed on hers and then the old lady shut her eyes peacefully.

It was a long night. Alex tried to persuade her to rest on the sofa he had moved close to the bed and she tried to coax him to do the same, but when both realised neither was going to budge they sat side by side in the shadowed room, talking occasionally but mostly dozing, an ease in their relationship that had never been there before.

'This is real life, isn't it?' he said abruptly at one point in the night when Isabella's breathing had become more shallow. 'All the tinsel and glitter of that crazy world I'm involved with, it doesn't mean a thing.'

'Do you really mean that?' she asked quietly, and he glanced at her from the corner of his eye, a touch of the old arrogance in his face.

'Of course I mean it,' he said flatly. 'I've got no illusions about some of the people I have to deal with both on a business and social level but that's life.' He shrugged slowly. 'My grandmother made sure from an early age that I knew the difference between right and wrong—on her terms, and frankly her terms are good enough for me. We don't always see eye to eye, of course,' he smiled slightly, 'but our values are the same.'

'But Susan?' She stopped abruptly and stared at him, horrified that she had blurted out the woman's name.

'Susan?' He stared at her, puzzled. 'What has Susan got to do with anything?' The tawny eyes fixed on her tightly.

'I thought you liked her,' she said quickly. 'People talk, you know...' Her voice drifted away helplessly.

'Oh, I know all right,' he said bitterly. 'If anyone knows, I do! Susan is an old friend, nothing more. I find the children delightful but I'm afraid their mother——' He stopped suddenly. 'Well, let's just say my grandmother's initial feeling about her many years ago proved itself valid.'

'Did it?' The surge of joy that swept through her was so strong that she lowered her eyes swiftly, afraid he would read her mind. Isabella had been scathing about Susan and he was saying he agreed with it!

'I'm afraid Isabella is not one of Susan's biggest fans,' he said drily. 'Let's just leave it at that, shall we?' He glanced down at her bent head and when he spoke again his voice was deep and soft. 'I've learnt that the best things in life are often the hardest to get, but when you succeed it makes all the effort and heartache worthwhile. The trick is to keep trying, not to give up even when it appears hopeless. Sometimes you have to step back a while, bide your time, but that's just tactics. Not defeat.'

'I see.' She stared at him, her violet eyes huge in the shadowed darkness.

'I doubt it,' he said huskily. 'But maybe you will one day.'

At some point in the night they must have both drifted off into a deeper sleep because the arrival of John with a pot of coffee at about six woke them suddenly. 'How is she?' Alex opened bleary eyes and peered up at John who was bending over the bed.

'*She* is much better, thank you, Alexander,' a feeble old voice croaked irritably from the depths of the covers. 'And please don't refer to me in the way you would to a female cat.'

'Grandmama?' As Alex rose and bent over the tiny figure Fabia joined him, and both breathed a sigh of relief at the pink tinge to the face that stared back at them crossly.

'Such a fuss about nothing,' Isabella wheezed testily, giving John a long sharp glance in the process. 'I told him not to call you—a little rest and I knew I'd be fine. I was trying to juggle my tablets,' she admitted with a slightly sheepish glance at her grandson. 'I get tired of taking all that lot every day; I thought I'd cut down on one or two.'

'Isabella!' Fabia stared at the old lady in horror. 'Don't you ever do that again. That's really stupid; you could have killed yourself.'

'Nonsense.' The bright black eyes had their sharpness back again. 'And it's brought you two here to see me, hasn't it?' The dark eyes held Fabia's in a long considering gaze. 'And you weren't going to come back, were you?'

'Of course she was,' Alex said easily, unaware of the message passing between the two women. 'And now we're going to have some breakfast while you rest. And behave yourself,' he added warningly as he took Fabia's arm. 'I mean it, Isabella.'

'Just like your grandfather,' the old lady muttered crossly. 'Always thought he knew best, too.'

'Mary has some bacon and eggs on the go, sir, if you'd like to go down,' John said softly. 'I'll stay with Miss Isabella for now.'

'Thanks, John.' Alex patted the old man's arm as they left and the lined face smiled back at him understandingly.

'What on earth is going on?' They had just finished breakfast and were sitting in weary silence staring out of the huge full-length windows of the breakfast-room into the cold white world outside when Alex's gaze sharpened on a small figure in the distance. Fabia had been feeling acutely uncomfortable for the last few minutes, regretting the intimacy that seemed to have sprung up between them as some of the old doubts and fears were resurrected in the cold light of day. He had asked her to come here for Isabella's sake—fact. He hadn't contacted her once since the Christmas break—fact. He was a very attractive man in a world of beautiful women—fact.

'That's one of my gardeners.' As Alex's voice interrupted her thoughts again she heard the note of concern in his voice. 'And he's only got one dog with him. They don't usually separate.'

They met the red-faced man on the doorstep and he took a moment to catch his breath before he spoke, Major bounding up to Alex with a bark of delight but then running halfway across the lawn before barking again loudly.

'We've lost one of the dogs, sir.' The man looked up at Alex anxiously. 'My lad took them for a short walk this morning before breakfast, knowing how things were in the house, and one of them didn't come back when he called.'

'Where did he take them?' Alex asked quickly as he turned back into the hall and reached for his coat.

'Down by Sabre Wood, sir.' The man raised a hand as Alex went to speak. 'I know, sir, I know. I told him not to go there but the lad's young and he forgot.'

Alex swore softly. 'Young be damned, Mike. That wood is lethal at the best of times with the bog and sudden drops in height. It's been a no-go area for years. There are stretches there I wouldn't like to wander into on a summer's day.' He turned to Fabia suddenly as if he had just remembered she was standing by his side.

'It's all right,' he said calmly. 'I'll be back shortly. Keep an eye on Isabella for me and don't tell her anything; she doesn't need another set-back.'

'Where are you going?' Her voice was shrill with fear but she didn't care.

'You know where I'm going,' he said quietly. 'Minor is out there somewhere, either in the wood or the surrounding fields. He could be hurt or worse. You don't expect me to leave him there, do you?'

'I wouldn't go, sir,' the gardener said at the back of them. 'There are some wicked drifts out there and——'

'That's enough, Mike,' Alex said coldly. 'You're going to worry the lady unnecessarily.'

'He could be dead already,' Fabia said desperately. 'You know he could.'

'Or waiting to be rescued,' Alex said softly. 'Listening, waiting, probably scared out of his wits. I can't leave him out there, Fabia, I'm sorry.' He had pulled on a large pair of wellington boots as he was talking and clicked his fingers at Major as he straightened. The big dog bounded immediately to his side. 'I'm tempted to leave him here for safety but he can probably guide me right to where Minor is,' Alex said slowly. 'I'll be back before you know it.' He touched her cheek gently with leather-clad fingers and then he was gone, down the steps into the snow, shouting orders at Mike as he went, with Major barking enthusiastically by his side.

'Alex . . .' She watched the two figures until they disappeared from sight and then started violently as Mary touched her shoulder gently.

'Come on in, lass, you'll catch your death,' the housekeeper said gently. 'I've made the fire up in Mr Alexander's sitting-room and you can stretch out on the sofa there until he comes back—unless you'd like to go upstairs for a rest?'

'No, I'll wait in the sitting-room,' Fabia said gratefully. It had Alex's presence stamped all over it, and somehow she needed that security just at the moment. She felt sick with tiredness.

She was convinced she wouldn't sleep a wink but the next time she opened her eyes it was early afternoon and the weather had worsened if anything. 'All the phone lines are down, Miss Fabia,' Mary said worriedly after Fabia had wandered into the kitchen to find Mary and Jenny in a huddle by the window. 'And the wind's getting up.' Fabia's stomach knotted with fear.

After a quick cup of coffee she went upstairs to Isabella's room to check on the old lady and was relieved to find she was almost her old self, sitting up in bed in a quilted bed-jacket with her hair brushed into order and her reading glasses perched on the end of her nose.

'Is Alexander awake yet?' Isabella asked as she entered the room. 'John said he was asleep.' Fabia glanced swiftly at the old butler sitting by Isabella's side.

'Not yet,' she said brightly. 'He shot back from America to see you, don't forget, and has only had cat naps over the last forty-eight hours. The poor man's exhausted.' As she spoke she glanced out of the window into the swirling, whining blizzard outside and her heart almost stopped with fear. He was tired and cold and he was out there!

She turned back to see Isabella looking at her strangely. 'What's the matter, Fabia?' the old lady asked quietly. 'Is there something I should know about?'

'Of course not.' Fabia forced an easy smile to her stiff lips.

'Come and sit by me, then,' Isabella said regally. 'I've got an old photo album here that might interest you.' As the afternoon darkened slowly into an ominous dusk her fear became all-consuming. It didn't help that Alex's face was staring back at her from the photo album! Alex as a rosy-cheeked baby; Alex looking heartbreakingly vulnerable as he smiled bravely at the camera on his first day at school, painfully smart in his new uniform; Alex in his first long trousers; Alex going to his first dance.

'Isn't that Susan?' Fabia peered more closely at one of the photos that featured a crowd of laughing teenagers grouped round a sports car.

'Yes,' Isabella said calmly. 'The car was Alexander's twenty-first present from me. Susan was his girlfriend then, you know.' She glanced at Fabia sharply. 'It was just after that that he finished with her, if I remember.'

'*He* finished with *her*?' Fabia asked slowly, remembering the women's conversation that night.

'Hasn't he told you?' Isabella asked quietly. 'He was no fool, my Alexander, even at that age. Susan wanted to marry a rich man and that's what she did—after Alexander had told her they were friends, nothing more.'

'I see.' A sudden gust of wind shook the window and Fabia reared anxiously from the bed. 'I'll just see if tea is on the way,' she said quickly to Isabella as she left the room, 'and stretch my legs a bit.'

'Look in on Alexander, would you?' Isabella called after her. 'I'd like to see him if he's awake.'

You'd like to see him? As she walked downstairs she realised it was now pitch-black and he was out there, in the worst storm for years, and she loved him. Strangely the realisation didn't terrify her, considering she had been fighting it for weeks. He had been gone for over eight hours now and besides that cold fact everything else paled into insignificance. Mary had told her the wood was about an hour's walk away—on a summer's day. Even allowing for double the time owing to the weather, and then the return journey, that still left four hours—four hours too long.

He had been mad to go, she had been mad to let him go, the world was mad! Why hadn't she contacted the police, ambulance, someone? She took a deep breath as her heart began to pound painfully. She loved him and he'd never know. He *was* dead. She felt it in her bones. Why had she looked at him, even for a moment, in the same light as Robin? Would Robin go out into arctic conditions looking for a human, let alone a dog? She sobbed suddenly into the stillness. This was judgement on her. She hadn't had the courage to reach out and trust her innermost heart when it had been telling her all along he was different. Maybe he would never love her, maybe she would just be another passing affair to him, but if she didn't give them the chance she would never know, would she? She ground her teeth in an agony of regret. Physical attraction was a start, wasn't it? Maybe she could *make* him love her, building on that?

She paced back and forwards, ignoring the sound of Isabella's bell overhead, until John appeared in the doorway, his severe face soft in his distress. 'I'm sorry, but Miss Isabella wonders what's keeping you,' he said apologetically as he glanced at her tear-washed face. 'Shall I tell her you'll be up shortly?'

'I can't, John, not yet.' She couldn't endure more small talk when her heart was being slashed into tiny pieces. 'Tell her I'm having a bath or a rest or something.'

'What possessed him to go out in this?' John murmured anxiously, forgetting his stiffness in the face of another crisis in less than twenty-four hours. 'The dog might have come home by itself. Did MacKay go with him?'

'Is that the man called Mike?' Fabia asked quietly and when the old man nodded she nodded herself in answer.

'Well, he couldn't have a better man with him for conditions like these,' John said comfortingly. 'Knows the area round here like the back of his hand. Mr Alexander will be all right, Miss Fabia, don't worry.'

Don't worry! As the old man disappeared upstairs she had the mad impulse to run out into the snow and keep running until she found him. For the first time she felt she knew exactly how the big cats felt at the zoo when they prowled round a tiny confining cage, growling with frustrated rage and helplessness.

When she heard the faint sound of a dog barking in the distance she experienced such a feeling of relief that for a moment everything swam in a dark hazy mist, and then as she lifted her head towards the sound her blood froze. There was just one dog barking. What if Minor had found his way home by himself and the others were lost out there?

She raced into the hall, pulling on her coat as she went and not stopping to slip her feet into boots. Her light shoes were soaked within seconds as she stood at the top of the snow-covered steps and then, as a large bulky figure in thick coat and wellingtons appeared round a corner in the drive with a dog bounding at his side, the feeling of indescribable relief was replaced by hot blinding rage such as she had never known before. She flew down the steps and across the lawns towards him, stumbling in the two feet of snow that had covered everything in a thick white blanket, but righting herself as her fury drove her forwards.

'You stupid, stupid man!' she cried over the few yards separating them as she neared his side. 'How could you have been so incredibly stupid? You could have died out there! Everyone's been worried to death!'

'You didn't tell my grandmother, did you?' His face was a dull grey colour and he was walking as though each step would be his last, but she was too enraged with painful relief to notice.

'No, I didn't tell her.' She reached his side as she spoke and beat on his chest angrily. 'But what about me?' she asked with each blow. 'How could you do this to me?'

He stared at her silently as she continued in her tirade, hot tears stinging the numbed coldness of her face as she ranted and raved her grief.

'Come here.' As he lifted her up into his arms she clung on to him as though she would never let him go, collapsing against his wet body with a little inarticulate cry of relief.

'I thought you were dead, Alex, I thought you were dead.' As he carried her towards the house he looked down into her face with a strange smile hovering on his lips.

'Would you have minded?' There was no mockery in his voice, just a deep hard question that she answered immediately.

'I'd have died too.'

He stopped again in the middle of the snow-covered lawns as more lights flashed on in the house when Mary and the others realised he was home. 'What does that mean? Explain.' As she buried her head against the roughness of his coat his voice was threaded with wonder as he spoke again. 'I love you, Fabia. I've loved you from the very minute I saw you in the middle of that room amid a crowd of awful people who paled into insignificance beside you. I couldn't believe it when you turned out to be a Mary-Lou.' He hugged her to him as he started walking again. 'And when I found out what sort of a trick you'd played on me I knew you were the only woman I'd ever love. So beautiful, so defiant, so touchingly fierce.'

'You didn't mind?' She stared up into his face.

'I minded like hell,' he said grimly. 'But it was too late then. The die had been cast, the Cade curse had struck again. You were the one I'd been waiting for all my life and you loathed the very ground I walked on!'

'Not really,' she whispered against his chest. 'I was fighting myself as much as you.'

'Well, you went the full ten rounds, angel-face,' he said wryly as he reached the bottom of the steps. 'Is there anything there for me?' He stopped again and looked down into her face. 'Tell me, I want to hear it. I want to know this is not a dream, that it's real. Tell me, Fabia.'

'I love you, Alex.' As she spoke the last black thread of bitterness was loosened and her heart broke out into the glorious light.

'You love me?' He clasped her to him again. 'That was worth turning into a block of ice to hear. I thought I was going to have a hell of a fight on my hands before I'd hear you say that but I wasn't going to give up. Weeks, months, years—I'd have waited. Not patiently, maybe, but I'd have waited.'

'There are things you've got to know, Alex.' As he put her down inside the hall he looked at her for a long moment and then touched her face gently.

'Nothing would make any difference to the way I feel about you but let me get out of these wet things and then we'll talk.'

'Minor?' She looked down at Major with a little start of guilt. 'You didn't find him? Oh, Alex——'

'We found him.' As Mary and John appeared in the hall, faces wreathed in smiles, he took the dry clothes from John's hands with a little gesture of thanks. 'He'd managed to fall down one of the pot-holes that damn wood is littered with and break his leg besides getting his other paw stuck in some tree roots. There was no way he could have freed himself. We took him to the vet's in the next village before we came back; that's where he is now. I tried to phone but the lines are down.'

She stood, just feasting her eyes on him as he spoke, and as he returned the look John and Mary glanced at each other and then retraced their steps, leaving the two of them alone.

'Come in here.' As he pulled her into his sitting-room she felt his shaking through the hand holding hers and pushed him towards the roaring fire with a little cry.

'Get your things off, Alex.'

'Music to my ears.' He smiled wickedly at her blushes as he stripped down to nothing, donning his dry clothes with mocking reluctance and then drawing her into his arms as they sat in front of the fire. Mary had placed a flask of hot coffee liberally laced with brandy by his chair and Fabia made him drink two cupfuls before she would relax on his lap, snuggling against him as she did so.

He kissed her until she was breathless but as their caresses grew more feverish she pushed him away slightly, putting her finger on his lips as she did so. 'I want to tell you something, to make you understand why I'm like I am.'

He listened silently while she told him about Robin, leaving nothing out, and his face was dark with rage when she finished. 'I'd give the world for five minutes alone with him,' he said grimly.

'It's over now,' she said with an overwhelming sense of relief that she really was free at last, free to love again, free to live again. 'I just wish I'd never met him, that's all.'

'The past is past,' he said gently. 'I don't care about it as long as you love me now. Any other men——'

'There haven't been any others,' she said quietly. 'You will be the first, Alex, the first and the last.'

'Oh, my love...' As he gathered her close the look on his face made her want to cry again, but within a few minutes weeping was the last thing on her mind...

* * *

'Kiss the bride, sir! We want a nice friendly wedding, now, don't we!' As titters of laughter greeted the photographer's quip Alex leant towards her, moving the soft white silk of her veil aside as he bent to whisper in her ear.

'What happened to the little lady who informed me she was going to wear black on her wedding-day?'

She smiled wickedly, content and gloriously fulfilled on this her special day, and as she caught Isabella's eye in the background she lifted up her dress to reveal a saucy black garter on the top of one slim, beautifully shaped leg. 'I was going to keep this till later, but if you insist...'

He laughed delightedly, his eyes devouring her as she stood beside him, exquisite in her wedding finery, and as the photographer called again he gathered her up into his arms, holding her aloft in triumphant victory before claiming her lips as the camera flashed.

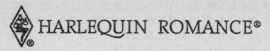 **HARLEQUIN ROMANCE®**

brings you

More Romances Celebrating Love, Families and Children!

Next month, look out for Emma Goldrick's new book,
Leonie's Luck, Harlequin Romance #3351
(a heart-warming story of romantic involvement between
Leonie Marshal and Charlie Wheeler, who marches
without warning—or permission—into her life!)

Charlie's nine-year-old daughter, Cecilia, who comes to
live with them—at Leonie's Aunt Agnes's invitation—is
somehow never far from what is going on and plays an
innocent part in bringing them together!

Available wherever Harlequin books are sold.